A Leisurely Stroll in the Dark
by
M. Alexander

Published by Sardonic Press

Cover Art by Monica Keszler

ACKNOWLEDGMENTS

This book wouldn't be what it is without the help of my sister Jennifer. She edited the first draft, pointed out plotholes, helped brainstorm solutions to said plotholes, and worked to improve my writing without sacrificing my "style." A subsequent draft was edited by my girlfriend Sanjukta, whose encouragement and feedback helped create a much more polished novel. I'd also like to thank my parents for understanding my need to take on all these different projects, and for the amazing opportunities they've afforded me.

CHAPTER ONE

Trenton walked across the street with his head down. This was pointless really. No matter what he did he would be completely recognizable. Still, he almost always kept his head down to avoid drawing unnecessary attention. Flicking his green eyes upward and side-to-side in order to take in the gleaming buildings and cars, he scanned the unnaturally clean street and the mass of people walking around him. Unfriendly faces kept their gaze plastered to the ground, too cautious to even lift their faces into the cooling afternoon air.

He continued down the other side of the street at a slightly faster pace in hope of distancing himself from the thickest part of the crowd, but not so fast that he would draw unwanted attention. He soon reached the plaza that held the Screens. Even with his gaze turned mostly downward, Trenton could still see the numerous images that moved across the different panes. For a moment, he was unable to resist his curiosity and lifted his head; hundreds of scenes from peoples' lives immediately filled his gaze.

Even with a TV in every room in the city, the government still *felt the need to build this shit.* Trenton didn't understand it, but he wasn't going to start complaining.

Once he managed to swallow his disgust over the spectacle being portrayed on the Screens, Trenton refocused on their design. They consisted of four gigantic television screens that bordered each side of the square. The lower lip of each screen hung about twenty-five feet above the ground and the transition from one to the next was seamless. Together they boxed in the crowds of people and blocked out the entire sky except for a tiny blue sliver directly above the square.

Trenton returned his attention to blending in and moved to the far left corner of the plaza. He neared a door that served as an entrance to one of the buildings directly behind the Screens. Only the first floor of the buildings was visible but Trenton knew they rose high above and figured there must be metal bars running from the buildings to the Screens in order to keep them in place. He reached out to turn the handle when a hand clenched down on his shoulder.

"You're early."

Trenton turned around slowly to see an exceptionally nondescript man standing before him.

"I couldn't wait," Trenton responded as calmly as he could.

"It's perfectly understandable that you're nervous. I'd be more worried if you weren't," the man said as he guided Trenton inside. The words sounded as if they should be reassuring, but somehow Trenton still had his doubts.

They entered a brightly lit hallway. The walls on each side were almost blindingly white, uninterrupted by any windows or doorframes. Trenton assumed there was a door at the end of the passage, but when he looked ahead he saw nothing except the smooth face of another wall. The man was right behind him, again with his hand on Trenton's shoulder.

Relentlessly, the man guided Trenton to the end of the hall. They stopped in front of the back wall, which was the exact same shade of white as the rest of the hallway. It looked smooth to the touch, while the others had a faintly textured appearance. The man reached around Trenton and pressed his palm flat against the face of the smooth wall. At first it appeared that nothing would happen, but then the wall (door?) slid aside to reveal another room much larger than the one they were currently standing in. The harsh brightness of the hallway was replaced with a juxtaposition of dark on light. The top half of the room was smothered in darkness, low enough that if Trenton stretched up a hand, his fingertips would disappear into the black. From head height and below, the light was enough to see by, if somewhat uneven; the source of the light was the thousands of monitors that covered every wall and filled the many aisles that ran the length of the room. Turning to the nearest row of screens, Trenton saw that each one was playing segments from a different person's life.

"So you're a teacher," the man said as he ushered Trenton farther into the room. "What do you teach again?"

Trenton was sure the man already knew the answer but felt required to reply. "History." The word barely came out. He cleared his throat. "I teach history." That was better.

"So you must know a great deal about how the world was before The Program came into being. Do you picture it as a better place? "

Trenton waited for him to answer his own question, knowing what the Government believed. But the man looked at him expectantly. Trenton forced his lips to form the words he wanted to hear. "Of course not. Millions of people went hungry and crime was the worst it's been in our history."

"That's right. And we got rid of both of those seemingly unsolvable issues in a matter of years. There's no law against teaching about the world before The Program, but it has come to our attention that you may be exaggerating the benefits of a world without The Program."

With another quick glance at the monitors, Trenton struggled to hold in his frustration. "Is this why you brought me here? To lecture me about my teaching practices?"

The man seemed completely unfazed by Trenton's aggressive demeanor. "Yes, and to remind you that we are always watching."

This only frustrated Trenton even more but he held back another angry remark and managed to regain his composure. "Thank you for that thoughtful reminder." He did his best to keep the sarcasm out of his voice and was mostly successful. "If there's nothing else?"

"There is one more thing actually. It seems you need a reminder as to the purpose of this Program. It exists so that every person in this city can live comfortably, with no fear of hunger or crime. There is no need for taxes to take the peoples' hard earned money because the Government has The Program to keep things running smoothly."

The man paused for second, waiting for his words to sink in. "We have nothing else to discuss. You may leave now." As the his last words faded away, the lights from the thousands of monitors clicked off in unison and a single light snapped on, illuminating a hallway that had previously been covered by darkness. Without waiting for further encouragement, Trenton entered the newly lit hallway, praying it led to an exit and the end of this frustrating encounter.

CHAPTER TWO

Minutes later, Trenton found himself standing outside – just as he had hoped. It was a bright, clear day. The only reminder of what had just transpired was the imprint of his fingernails in the palms of his hands. Around him, people went about their lives as they had for thousands of years. Well, it wasn't quite the same, but they did a good job of pretending it was.

Trenton started walking; he didn't know where he was going, only that he could no longer stand being next to a building that was so closely tied to The Program. He quickly realized that he had not exited the building in the same square that held the Screens. Instead, he was on the edge of a park.

As he approached, the park resembled those found in the old cities of which Trenton taught. But as Trenton walked closer, he saw how each plant was completely green, and each shrub perfectly pruned. Stranger still[1], there was not a single weed in the park. Even with advances in herbicides, weeds still sprang up everywhere. Except here. And in every other government owned park. Shaking his head, he made his way through the park. He had thought that he would start to cool off once he left behind the brightly lit monitors and the disquieting government official. However, with each step his anger only grew and by the time he reached the middle of the park, it threatened to erupt. He had buried this anger for years, thinking it would go away, that it wasn't worth wasting his life to act on it.

---

[1] It wasn't strange to Trenton, but it certainly wasn't natural.

Taking a deep breath, he formed a bare-bones[1] plan to resolve the cause of his anger (he had learned this technique through trial and error back when he was nine or ten. If he hadn't come up with a way of handling his disaster of a family, things would have turned out much worse).

Now that he had resolved to fight back, his anger dissipated and he was able to make it through the rest of the park without revealing his frustration to the cameras that watched from every angle. He had no idea how to return home from wherever he was, so he tapped his thumb twice on the piece of metal that encircled his pointer finger, and said, "take me home."

Immediately, the holographic screen popped up, seemingly independent from the ring on his finger. He used his right hand to position the screen so that he could still see the scenery in front of him as well as the directions indicated on the screen. After a few quick turns and a couple narrow-but-quite-safe back alleys, he found his way to a Public Transport System station, commonly referred to as a PTS station, and descended the stainless steel stairs into the city's greatest achievement. There was not a hint of dirt to be found and the walls shone with reflected light. People moved in a steady stream, never slowing. Each person spoke a few words into the empty air[2] and then strode on to the next available shuttle.

Trenton moved forward with the crowd, gesturing with his hand to dissolve the hologram display he had used for directions. He then tapped his thumb against the side of his pointer finger where his ring rested and said, once again, "take me home."

A Pod rose out of the ground in front of him and without pausing, he stepped inside. The door slid shut behind him as Trenton sat down on the leather couch that lined the edge of the Pod. The walls were an off-white and the couch the color of dark chocolate. He felt the vehicle accelerate and a few minutes later he was standing outside another PTS station, just a few blocks from his house. Walking the remaining distance to his apartment, he debated how to begin his attack on the government without getting caught within minutes of making a move. Nothing useful came to mind, but it had been a long day. *I'll think about this more tomorrow*, he thought.

[1] Ok, basically non-existent. It involved fighting back against The Program by joining the Resistance. Which was easier said than done.

[2] They spoke the names of places in the city (or maybe they were saying gibberish and wouldn't get very far) which was picked up by the ring on their finger. The ring communicated with the station, arranging for a Pod to pick them up, using their exact location in the station and their destination.

Trenton exhaled an almost inaudible sigh of relief when he finally reached the door to his building. He had half-expected to be stopped on the way back from that bizarre meeting, and only now unclenched his fists and felt his shoulders relax slightly. He entered the lobby, barely noticing the red and white marble tiles as his leather shoes thumped with each step. If Trenton had looked up from his shoes, he would have noticed the giant chandelier that hung from the vaulted ceiling, sparkling in the artificial light. But of course he did no such thing. Trenton refused to notice the intricate murals that decorated each wall. And though he still didn't look up, he could *feel* the small black dot that marked the cameras at the top of each corner of the room, staring down at him.

Trenton reached the staircase at the far-end of the room, and climbed up the three flights of stairs without hesitation. As he approached the door and tapped his thumb against his ring, it slid open. "What time is it?" Trenton asked, too tired (or lazy) to even check his ring.

"5:34 pm." The reply came from the middle shelf of a cabinet, where a black, metal speaker sat comfortably. The true source of the response was the ring on his finger, which connected to virtually everything in his home, and quite a few other things besides.

Did that whole fiasco really only take two hours? I guess time slows down when you're talking it up with government officials.

Without another thought, Trenton slipped into bed, and was asleep 97 seconds later.

CHAPTER THREE

Trenton opened his eyes. His alarm went off, an annoying buzz starting to fill the air. He got out of bed and the alarm quieted at once. As he made his way to the bathroom, ideas for the lectures he was scheduled to give today began to percolate alongside breakfast choices and post-work plans. On the edge of his thoughts, possible ways of fighting The Program took root. Leaving his ring on the small table by the side of the entrance, he walked into the bathroom, firmly closing the door behind him. They may never show footage of anyone in the bathroom, but Trent was sure they had cameras there. Yet even if they did, why make it any easier for them?

After an 8.5 minute shower and 1.25 minutes of brushing his teeth, for a combined time in the bathroom of 10.25 minutes (including toweling and transit), Trenton exited the bathroom, nearly ready to start the day. (The astute observer would note that the disposal of bodily substances was conspicuously absent from the official time-log).

He quickly got dressed, pulling a non-descript button-down shirt over his head and buttoning the top button, which had been previously left undone to allow his head access. His black hair was unyielding in its pursuit of chaos, his jeans pulled up to his waist, sans-belt. Remembering to slip the ring back on his finger, he then left his room and the building, making his way to the nearest PTS station.

As Trent entered the underground tunnel he tapped his finger and said "Take me to the schools." The familiar sphere-shaped pod rose from the ground in front of him and Trent stepped inside. Eight minutes (and 2 seconds) later he exited the pod and climbed the stairs to the outdoors, the Schools rising up in front of him. They were made up of three towers arranged like an arrowhead pointing towards the heart of the city. Each tower was a perfect cylinder with thousands of curved windows reflecting the early morning sun.

Trenton reached his classroom a few minutes early and strode into the room. Only a few students had taken their seats, with many more on the way. This class consisted mostly of 13 and 14 year-olds, but Trenton also taught a class for only the most advanced students, the majority of which were 20 and 21 year-olds.

The rest of the students began to trickle in as Trent took his time writing the schedule for the day on the board. His ring gave him full access to the board, allowing him to not only write on it, but also to call up any recorded piece of history deemed appropriate by the Schools (and therefore the government). He could find virtual reproductions of texts dating back centuries, and enlarge them for the class to see. He could show footage from wars or scientific breakthroughs. Almost anything he could think of could be brought up and used to teach the class - just as long as he remembered what he'd been told when he started teaching, and reminded of just yesterday.

With an almost inaudible sigh, he resigned himself to teaching only the accepted material from now on. If he wished to fight the government, he couldn't risk drawing any more attention to himself.

He cast a glance at the side of the room where a small screen kept track of the time. 8:00 am exactly.

Still facing the board, Trenton asked, "Does anyone remember what we discussed yesterday?"

The room faded into silence, the students still half asleep. Trenton turned around to see a single hand hesitantly enter the air.

"Go ahead James." Trenton gestured to the boy.

" We had just started talking about the Depression of the 2020's."

"That's right." Trent tapped the board, bringing up various images from the era. "This was a terrible time. People starved, people stole, people killed. It eventually got so bad that in the year 2031, the government decided to set up a network of cameras to stop the crimes. The cameras enabled them to identify any criminal and assign the appropriate punishment. As a result, crime became virtually non-existent. However, the majority of people were still so poor they couldn't afford a decent meal." Pictures of emaciated bodies filled the board.

"Then one man had a brilliant idea," Trenton continued, keeping his tone neutral. "If the government made use of the footage of peoples' lives, they could earn money to both maintain the city and rescue the population from starvation. So in the year 2033, they began a trial run, selling any interesting segments of their citizens' lives to the local cable networks. It was a massive success, earning enough money for the stars of the segments that they managed to climb out of poverty. The extra money also served to rebuild the crumbling infrastructure of the city, generating jobs and ultimately serving to jumpstart the economy, leading to a better quality of life for everyone within the city limits."

Mentally Trenton added, *Not that we had any choice but to go along with it.*

The rest of the class continued in a similar manner, with Trenton spewing praise for how The Program had saved the city from poverty and destruction, and the students sitting behind their desks with slightly bemused expressions spread across their faces. They said nothing, but Trenton knew they were disappointed by his sudden shift in attitude towards the government. Or to put it bluntly, his level of bullshit.

Around mid-day, Trenton made his way to a nearby sub-shop for lunch. He had one more class afterwards and then he was free to iron out a plan to fight back against The Program. He sat in the straight-backed aluminum chair, eating his sandwich. He ate with a quick efficiency, barely noticing the taste. When he had only a few bites remaining, the holographic display in the corner, commonly referred to as an H-display, suddenly caught his eye. The sound was turned down low so that only a whisper reached his ears, but the screen made it all too clear what was taking place.

A young woman sat in a plain steel chair, completely surrounded by holographic displays. These displays played back her entire life; there was no filter, no sensor, nowhere to hide. Trenton couldn't make out what was being said – there was only the vague murmuring of a gravely voice – but he'd heard it enough times before to get the idea.

The bodiless whisper of a growl continued, listing the crimes the girl had committed. Up until this instant, she had maintained her composure, but as her expression changed, Trenton knew her punishment was being relayed, and it was as expected.

The camera panned around the nameless criminal, capturing her wide eyes and trembling body. Two men entered the scene, carrying large briefcases.   They set them on a nearby table and began removing the required tools.

As was customary, they began with the fingers, slowly sawing through them at the second joint, one at a time. The girl began to scream, the sharp echoes disquieting in spite of – or perhaps because of – their unnaturally low volume. The top half of her right index finger wobbled for a second, then fell to the floor. The men silently moved to the next finger. This continued for 4.3 minutes, not that the subject had any use for this fact. One would imagine she was a bit pre-occupied.

Next they moved to her face, first taking a short commercial break as they set up the necessary tools.

They worked on her face for another 6.1 minutes. This was an area ripe with opportunity and so took slightly more time than the hands.

When they were finally finished, the girl slouched in her chair and the camera changed angles to get a better view of the result.

In the place where her nose should have been was a jagged bloody hole. All that remained of her left eye was a black charred mass, still smoking slightly. The shattered remains of her teeth kept her mouth from closing, leaving the girl's face locked in a constant scream.

And with that, The Program terminated.

Without a word, Trenton pushed his way out of the building.

CHAPTER FOUR

The next morning, Trenton woke early and remembered something that instantly lightened his mood: today was Saturday. As a teacher, his only official work for the weekend consisted of grading any assignments due in the last few days. There was only one such assignment, an essay on the pitfalls of American Capitalism at the beginning of the 21st century. The paper had been due by 10:00 pm last night. Trenton decided to check for the inevitable stragglers.

He moved from his bed to his desk, a distance of about 4 feet, 2.5 inches. In response to Trenton's position at the desk, his ring automatically brought up a virtual keyboard and monitor to facilitate his work.

He quickly navigated the various menus with his hands, flipping through any messages he may have missed while sleeping, checking the weather, and finally, opening the log of homework submissions. Scanning through the names he noticed one submission at 10:01, a full minute late. Feeling merciful, Trenton overrode the grade deduction, changing it from -10% to only -5%. He noticed that one submission was completely missing. He wasn't so generous with that student.

Grabbing the virtual monitor with his hand, Trenton stood and walked into the bathroom to brush his teeth and shoot the porcelain. He positioned the screen in the corner of the room and turned on his favorite broadcast, going about his business (somewhat literally).

After he finished in the bathroom, he moved to the common area, once again bringing the screen with him, using his hands to stretch it to a much larger size. The walls were painted a deep blue, with a myriad of lounging options scattered around the room. He chose a seat in a leather recliner, letting the sound and light from the screen wash over him, lost in thought.

He needed to find a way to discretely contact a few of his friends he had long suspected of being members of the Resistance. He knew any direct approach would simply draw both of them under suspicion (and in Trenton's case, any further suspicion would likely leave him missing a few important things – fingers, for example). No, what he needed was a subtle approach that would be obvious to only existing members of the Resistance. But since he *wasn't* a member yet, this made things substantially more difficult.

On the screen in front of him, a new show began, and Trenton recognized it as one of the longest-running shows on The Program. It featured a skinny Chinese man who wasted his time acting ridiculous and squandering the vast sums of money The Program brought him. A lot of people enjoyed his cocky demeanor and the strange situations he got himself into. Various scenes from his life played almost everyday, with a new episode every Tuesday and Friday night.

Trenton flicked his hand, changing the channel.

A soap opera supposedly starring real people, but with obviously staged drama flashed on.

He flicked to a new channel.

A far too legitimate love-scene.

Another flick.

A man shooting someone with a shotgun. That wasn't fake blood.

Flick.

A grown man crying in his bathtub-

Trenton tapped his ring, ending the parade of images. In the newfound silence, he sat, head tilted slightly back, eyes unseeing. In this moment, he looked far older than his 31 years. His mind wandered unbidden to vague memories of the time before cameras filled every room and the streets held not a hint of disorder. Before people made their living selling their lives away, and before every man, woman, and child had enough to eat.

With a conscious effort, Trent returned to his current problem, leaving those thoughts for later. What could he do? A note might be possible if he managed to write it shielded from any cameras. But if it were discovered, the results would be dire. He could try hinting at wanting to join the Resistance to those he strongly believed to be involved, but if he were too direct or if he was wrong, they might go to the police, or The Program might investigate them both.

The one thing Trenton knew for sure was that he had to do something, even if it resulted in his own public trial. So he sat in his chair for almost an hour, turning the screen back on at a very low volume so as not to appear too odd for the camera that he knew was still watching. No brilliant ideas flooded his mind, no happy accident led to a solution[1].

After this less than fruitful session, he decided to go for a walk to clear his head. It was a little before midday when Trenton walked out onto the street. The sun hid behind a few stray clouds and a handful of people strolled about, driven by a lack of purpose only common on weekend mornings.

Walking aimlessly, Trenton soon came across a vacant bench, facing the opening of a well-manicured park. He sat down, and not a minute later a shout rang out behind him,

"Alex! HEY!" The owner of the voice drew closer as Trenton twisted around on the bench to see his sister staring back at him. She wore a billowing dress in the current fashion, her long brown hair obscuring part of her face.

With a hint of a grin, Trenton responded, "I'm glad to hear you can yell as loud as ever."

"Well you were sitting there, oblivious as can be. Made me crank up the volume."

"I'm just not used to hearing people call me Alex. No one besides you and dad call me that," he said, gesturing for her to sit. She didn't.

Instead she rolled her eyes. "Sorry *Trenton*, I forgot how in love you are with our last name. Just as long as you don't start calling me that."

"Don't worry, *Jessica*, I won't. So what are you doing on this very average Saturday morning? I mean besides following me."

"Going to get brunch actually. I'm starving," she said. "Wanna join me?"

"Only if there's bacon," Trent said.

There was bacon.

■■

[1] After all this is not some pop novel, this is serious shit.

The rest of the weekend passed by all too quickly, as weekends tend to do, and Trenton found himself falling asleep Sunday night, wondering where the last 47 hours and 11 minutes had gone.

Or maybe he wasn't wondering about that exact span of time, but that *was* the moment Trenton arrived home Friday night, marking it as the true start of his rather uneventful weekend.

But I digress…

In only a few minutes, Trent was asleep.

At first he dreamed of nothing in particular, his mind flitting between settings and circumstances at an unimaginable rate. But then the spinning wheel of thoughts slowed and his mind settled on a strange scene. A scene that is almost as uncomfortable to read as it was to experience.

The first thing Trenton noticed when he opened his eyes was his own face staring back at him. The second thing he noticed was the thick darkness that hung in the air. He refocused on what he naively assumed to be a mirror held in front of him, and shivered. Where there had been one face, there were now five, not five but ten, not ten but a hundred. Then a thousand faces – exact replicas of his own – stared back at him, expressionless. They formed walls on either side of him, leaving only a narrow dark corridor of empty space.

A guttural cry rang out behind him, but Trenton could see nothing besides the floating heads, gray in the darkness.

Another cry, closer.

Trenton started running, away from the sound, down the hallway. On either side, the walls of identical faces reflected back at him, silent in their judgment. He ran faster, the cries getting closer with each second. Sweat iced his forehead, and his legs burned. A cold certainty filled him: when that *thing* caught up with him, he would face something far worse than death.

Over his labored breathing he heard a scraping sound behind him and risked a glance over his shoulder: a black mass rose up, its features slathered in darkness. Trenton ran faster, the image burned into his mind, spurring him on.

Ahead, he could make out a distant light. It grew closer and closer, but that *thing* was still right behind him. In what felt like an eternal instant, Trenton lunged forward, out of the face-lined hallway and into the day. Still running, he glanced behind him: the beast was nowhere in sight. With a relieved laugh he collapsed on the hard ground, the cement was warm under his fingers. He looked up, taking in the tall buildings and immaculate streets. It was the city, but something wasn't right.

As his breathing slowed, he heard it. Or rather he heard nothing at all. No people chatted as they walked the streets, no cars grumbled on their way around the city, no wind whistled between the buildings. There was nothing, and Trenton was nothing, just a tiny speck in the vast expanse of metal, glass, and concrete.

He pushed himself to his feet, painfully aware of his own insignificance. He started walking, weaving his way between buildings, exploring the empty shell of his city. Soon Trenton recognized the feeling: he was being watched. Everything else was gone, but the cameras that littered the city remained.

CHAPTER FIVE

It was a Monday morning like any other. Trenton brushed his teeth, ate breakfast, traveled to school, joined the Resistance, and taught American history to his first batch of students. The story of his breakfast is quite an interesting one. He had an omelet with peppers, onions, and mushrooms, as well as a side of bacon. Fascinating.

But the other story of interest, the one that will most greatly shift the course of Trenton's life, is how he joined the Resistance.

He strongly believed one of his few close friends to be involved in the fight against the government. So while Trenton was in his just-big-enough-to-not-be-cramped kitchen, eating his delicious omelet, he wrote three words on a scrap of toilet paper he had taken from the bathroom and placed up his sleeve.

I want in.

He had cleverly positioned himself so that his back was to the one camera in the kitchen, and his ring was still on the table outside the bathroom. He was as confident as was possible that no camera had glimpsed his actions. That had to be enough.

He then discreetly placed the note in his pocket, finished his breakfast, and walked out the door. He knew it might be days before he ran into his friend and could deliver the note, but in this small thing, he was lucky. He was just entering the PTS station on his way to work when a familiar-shaped head entered his field of view.

"Hey Jason!" Trent said.

The owner of the head turned around in surprise. Then smiled in recognition. "Trent! Good to see you. It's been a few days." They moved over to the side of the station to avoid affecting the steady stream of commuters passing by.

"Yeah I've been meaning to get in touch, but it's been a little crazy. You want to share a pod?" Trenton asked, hands in his pockets.

"Sure, but I'm actually in a rush today so I'll have to get out first. Can't be late for my meeting," Jason said.

"Ok." They entered a Pod together, not needing to say anything at all. They're destinations were both already stored in their rings, and they had been overheard (of course) saying they would share a ride.

They spent the few minutes before Jason's stop on the comfortable leather couch, talking about what they had planned for the rest of the week. Then Jason's ring dinged and the Pod came to a halt.

They shook hands as Jason said, "We should grab a beer sometime this week."

"Definitely." Then Trent waved him off, knowing how busy he was.

With a nod, Jason rushed off to his meeting, and that was that. However, the attentive reader would remember the note in Trenton's pocket, and would wonder if they did more than just exchange farewells.

■■■

The next few days were uneventful, even by the standards of someone involved in education. Trenton taught, ate, and slept, and little else. He did his best to act as if nothing had changed, and tried not to worry about the note he may or may not have given to his friend Jason. As time wore on, this became more and more difficult.

There were a multitude of possibilities as to why there had been no response. One was that it took time for the Resistance to communicate and to get in contact with people. This was reasonable because of the extensive infrastructure of cameras they had to circumvent. Another possibility was that they had decided they couldn't trust him. For all they knew Trent could be a spy for the government, although Trenton hoped Jason would vouch for him.

Of course the most obvious was that Jason was not actually part of the Resistance. If this was the case, Trent had to hope that Jason would stay quiet; if Jason reported him, the outcome wouldn't be too pretty – although some do claim to see a sort of macabre beauty in what the government does to traitors of The Program.

After a week had passed, Trenton decided to stop actively worrying about the whole ordeal since he no longer had even a modicum of control over the situation. Instead he tried enjoying the present, but he never felt like he could fully relax[1].

He eventually grabbed that beer with Jason, neither one of them mentioning anything more delicate than the score of the latest soccer game. The Pirates lost 4 to 3 in the last 67 seconds of the game if you really must know.

It was nice to unwind a little, even if much was left unsaid.

Trenton continued to teach a more slanted version of history, always careful to ensure he was casting The Program and the government in a better light. His students continued to sulk silently in response. But they wouldn't make an issue of it. Any verbal outcry would attract unwanted attention, especially if it could be construed as speaking out against The Program.

In an effort to take his mind off of his current situation, Trent decided to go climbing the following weekend. This was a rare occurrence, and well overdue. One call to his friend Chris and 47.3 hours later, Trenton stood at the foot of an eighty-foot-tall cliff face.

"This'll be quite a climb," Chris said, coming up behind him. "I'm still surprised the government doesn't mind us coming out here." "Oh they'd only care if we tried to leave completely. Technically we're still in the outer limits, where we can't bother anyone besides the occasional farmer."

"Yeah true. I bet they have killer security though." Chris looked around as if he could see anything besides trees and rocks.

They had already set up the rope at the top of the cliff, and were just about ready to start climbing.

Trent looked at Chris. "You want to go first?"

"Nah you did most of the work setting up, you get to go first. I'll belay," Chris responded. He took hold of the rope hanging down from the cliff and looped it through a small metal device attached to his harness. This allowed him to easily tighten or loosen the rope, depending on Trent's climb.

Trenton took the other end of the rope and tied a figure-8 knot to the front of his own harness. He approached the cliff-face and began to climb, skipping the usual dialogue that's meant to accompany the beginning of every climb. Chris saw him start up the wall and assumed

---

[1] Not that this was anything new, but he was aware of it all the same.

the correct stance, one foot in front of the other with both hands on the rope. The finger-holds were nothing more than tiny cracks or bumps in the rock, and Trenton was careful not to move too quickly. He placed both feet and one hand in a (somewhat) stable position before reaching above him with his other hand. Then he brought both feet up and repeated his original motion. Trenton could feel the slight tug on his harness as Chris pulled the rope tight after every move, ensuring that any fall would end long before Trent hit the ground.

"Remind me again why you don't wear a helmet? Chris's bare head called up to him. Chris was belaying, and so was relatively safe except for the miniscule chance of a rock breaking free from the cliff as Trenton was climbing.

"You know why. The breeze on my head helps keep me cool." *Plus what's the point if there's no danger at all?*

Contrary to what your grandmother may say, rock climbing, when done properly, is extremely safe.

If there's no risk, I might as well be sitting at home watching someone else climb this piece of rock, Trenton thought.

His attention was pulled from his thoughts by the sight of an overhang jutting out of the wall above him. He would have to either jump up and grab onto the outer edge, or try and maneuver around it. He took a minute to decide, body hugging the wall, relatively secure in his current position. Curious, he looked down and saw Chris and the rocky ground a full stomach-dropping distance below.

"I'm going to jump to that ledge," Trent called down.

"Ok!" Chris tightened his hold on the rope and set his feet.

Looking up at the overhang, Trenton felt his breath quicken slightly and the rest of the world dropped away. Without another thought, he propelled himself up and away from the cliff face, arms outstretched.

For just a moment, he hung in the air, teeth clenched, eyes focused. His hands reached for the ledge and clamped down but his body swung outwards, threatening to dislodge him. Desperately he hung on, fighting his screaming muscles. His body started to swing back towards the rock but Trent kicked out with his legs, slowing himself enough that he was able to pull his knee up next to his hands and claw his way over the ledge.

Drawing in a shuddering breath, he tried to piece his mind back together. He glanced down at is hands – they were covered in blood.

CHAPTER SIX

As days turned into weeks, there was still no answer. Trenton became convinced that his note had never reached the Resistance. He briefly considered trying again, but knew a second attempt would be pretty much asking to have his limbs separated from his body.

And having failed in his one chance to fight against The Program, Trenton slowly lost hope. The time he didn't spend teaching or keeping himself alive, he spent in a dazed stupor sitting in front of his hologram, seeing nothing.

Still, Trenton was smart. He kept up pretenses remarkably well, and only a keen observer with far too much time on their hands would have noticed the difference. He had watched a fair amount of television before all this, so that raised no questions. When he was teaching, he was by and far his usual self, though he of course still focused only on the benefits of The Program and none of its many shortcomings. He still met up with the occasional friend; they could tell something wasn't quite right, but they didn't mention anything, guessing it was something better left unsaid.

Then one day Trenton found himself at school, in the middle of lecturing when he trailed off. He racked his brain but couldn't remember how he had gotten there or even what he had been saying. He looked to the board but it was largely unhelpful.

"Ben! What I have been talking about these last five minutes?" he asked a student who had his head down on his desk.

Ben stared blankly back at him.

"That's what I thought. Please listen from now on." Trent pointed to another student. "Alysse, inform Ben of what he missed."

Alysse sat up a little straighter in her chair. "You were discussing the treatment of the Native Americans both when the settlers from Europe first came, and then after the settlers had kicked them out."

"Very good, Alysse, thank you." Trent continued on as if nothing had happened. It was only later when he got home that he let any hint of his distress bubble to the surface.

He sat with the holographic display on, wondering if he was losing his mind. When he silently asked his magic conch shell, it said "Signs point to yes." But who gives a fuck what a plastic shell thinks?

After Trenton's mental lapse the weekend seemed impossibly far away. When it did finally arrive, he had partially recovered and was doing his best to give his mind a much-needed rest. He spent all of Saturday walking around the city, thinking up lives for the people he passed on the streets, and wondering if they were as miserable as he was. Sunday he spent with his sister, discussing ancient[1] history.

Another week passed, with Trenton finally achieving a sort of equilibrium. He had come to accept the lack of response to his note, if not completely forget about it.

Around noon during another day at the Schools, he took his lunch break at the sub shop. He ordered his sandwich, placing his ring in his pocket in anticipation of the mess he would undoubtedly make. A few minutes later the chef handed him his chicken-parmesan sub, the same as every other day. But today, Trenton felt a tickle on the palm of the hand that cradled the sandwich.

Keeping his face as steady as he could, he made his way to a table, sat down, and casually placed his hand in his pocket (the one *not* containing his ring) and transferred the tiny slip of paper that had been tickling his palm. He forced himself to eat slowly, as if nothing had happened. And for the rest of the day he fought to maintain that image. Nothing had happened.

It was nearly 5 pm when Trent finally arrived home, worn out from suppressing his excitement all day. He decided to wait until tomorrow night to read the note, knowing he might be watched extra closely if anyone had noticed something odd about his behavior or had seen him put something in his pocket at lunch. It would be difficult to wait, but it was best to be cautious.

The next day passed by at an agonizingly slow pace. At times Trenton swore the clock was actually counting backwards. Maybe he had

---

[1] Not literally.

inadvertently discovered the secret to time travel. Or maybe he was going nuts again. The two options seemed equally likely.

When night had fallen and Trenton was once again back in his apartment, he tried thinking about the last 13 hours and 4.3 minutes, but he remembered nothing except the face of the digital clock, slowly moving forward and backward in time.

Setting aside that troubling thought, Trent went about preparing dinner: leftover spaghetti and meatballs. He made himself a big plate and stuffed it in the microwave, leaving it inside until the machine beeped, letting him know the food was at the optimal temperature.

He sat down at the small table in the corner of the kitchen, back to the camera and ring in his pocket. He began to eat slowly, occasionally glancing at the H-Display he had arranged on the far wall. About 3 minutes and 31 seconds into the meal, Trenton casually reached into his pocket while turning to look at the screen. When he looked back to his food, he placed the note right on his plate, next to the bulk of the food, his body still shielding the camera's view.

He looked down at the note, continuing to eat all the while.

It read: *The Black Cat is a good place for a drink.*

Trenton had been to that pub on occasion, so it wouldn't be too suspicious if he started showing up there more frequently. As soon as Friday night came around, he knew where he'd be.

He covered the note with some pasta and sauce and used a spoon and fork to eat the rest of his meal, note and all.

CHAPTER SEVEN

Trenton ambled down the street like there was no rush, like the blood wasn't pounding in his eardrums. He even stopped at the less congested street corners to enjoy the cool breeze that drifted from building to building. The sun had just set, leaving only a whisper of light in its wake, and the streets were blissfully quiet. Only a few cars patrolled the streets with most everyone traveling on foot, on their way to get a drink. Or dinner. Or whatever else people do on a Friday night.

As Trenton approached the door to The Black Cat he feared he might actually burst from the excitement, but kept up a relaxed appearance. He took a deep breath, and then opened the door.

A blast of music and a hundred indistinct voices rushed through the open door and onto the barren sidewalk beyond as Trenton stepped into the room. Weaving between bodies, he inched his way closer to the bar. He nodded to the bartender and sat down on the only vacant stool. He ordered a drink and waited for something to happen. An hour drifted by. Then three. Trent still sat isolated at the crowded the bar, waiting. Midway through his fifth beer he realized a sobering truth: no one was coming tonight. Finishing his drink, he headed home, only stumbling twice on his way.

■■

In the morning Trenton woke, remembered the previous night, and felt a fresh wave of disappointment wash over him. His throat was as dry as expected, and his head wasn't too great either. Groaning, he reached automatically for the glass of water he kept next to his bed, but his hand grabbed nothing but air.

"Damn alcohol, makes you forget the important things," he muttered to himself.

His brain felt stiff as he rolled out of bed and shuffled to the bathroom. His next stop was the kitchen, in search of that missing glass of water. The search didn't take long, ending with Trenton drinking nearly half a gallon of water.

Trenton considered going back to the *Cat* again tonight but knew he shouldn't; he never went to a bar two nights in a row. He sighed.

"What time is it?" he asked the air.

The air responded[1], "It's 11:14 am."

Just enough time to do nothing all day.

■■

After some amount of nothing later – 13 hours and 21.2 minutes of nothing, to be exact – Trenton fell into a restless sleep. He dreamed of iron bars and the same black mass that had chased him out into the empty city. He'd had similar dreams a lot these past few weeks. When he woke, he was left with a bone-numbing coldness and a (rational) fear that something was watching him in the darkness.

He turned on the light, but remained in bed. He lay there for a while, thinking. He had just about gotten control of his life when the response had finally appeared. He couldn't let himself slip back into the fog that had overtaken him before. He had to stay positive and go through the motions until he was able to actively contribute to the Resistance, however long that took.

With that decided, Trenton spent the rest of the day being as productive as possible. Lounging around without a purpose would only leave him more time to feel sorry for himself. He cleaned the house, something that, like the typical bachelor, he had avoided for some time now. He shopped around for various necessary items, like clothes, food, and a bobble-head of our first president, George Washington. As I said, essential items.

The next day was Monday and Trenton faced it head on with admirable aplomb. He was slightly more energetic during his lectures, and time no longer seemed to fluctuate haphazardly, which he took as a good sign.

A month passed in a similar fashion, with Trenton lounging at The Black Cat more weekends than not. By this time he had met more

---

[1] Well technically his ring responded but the air sounds more poetic don't you think?

than a few people at the bar, although no one appeared to have more than a friendly interest in him.

One night he was sitting at his usual spot, chatting with a sandy-haired neighbor, when he decided to order some wings.

"You want some?" Trenton asked his neighbor, whom he decided to refer to as Cleft in honor of his impressive cleft chin.

"Oh man, I never turn down free wings," Cleft grinned at him, putting his ring in his pocket to avoid the incoming mess. Trent did the same.

As the food arrived, a man bumped into Trenton from behind, causing his stool to teeter precariously. Trent grabbed hold of the bar to steady himself as the drunken man apologized repeatedly. "It's fine," Trenton assured him, and the man wandered away. The food was uninjured and that was all that mattered.

Having remained silent throughout the encounter, Cleft began speaking at a low enough volume that anyone more than a foot away would be unable to hear over the roar of the room. He said, "I think it's time you got more involved with us." His posture was relaxed and his expression friendly.

Trenton was careful not to react. Was this finally it? He asked, "What do you mean?"

"I think you know," Cleft responded. "You don't have to worry about your ring listening in right now. I've got that covered."

"What do you mean you have it covered?"

"I can't explain right now, but you have to either trust me or go home."

Trent thought for two seconds. He had a feeling that if he went home, he wouldn't get another chance. So it wasn't much of a choice. "Ok. Tell me what you need me to do."

The man smiled. "We're starting to do some 'repairs' on some of the cameras around the city. There's been word that some have stopped working entirely."

"And?"

"We know you like to stroll around the city most weekends. Next weekend, you're going to drop some harmless little rocks in the square that holds the Screens, and by the entrance to as many PTS stations as you can, including the one on 5th street. Then you go home. That's all."

"I think I can handle that," Trent said, taking a gulp of beer to wash down the wings. "But how will I get the rocks?"

"Check your pocket."

Trenton casually placed a hand on his thigh and felt a slight bulge that hadn't been there at the beginning of the night. Guess that drunken collision earlier in the night hadn't been an accident after all.

The rest of the evening passed by without further mention of the Resistance. The two men drank and laughed and then drank again. Trenton headed home around 12:46, wobbly as a whale.

CHAPTER EIGHT

As drunk as he had been, Trent remembered virtually every word Cleft had said during their (hopefully) private conversation. He had been given a real job. He had no idea what his job really *was*, but he was ecstatic nonetheless.

The first thing Trenton did that day was to fold up his discarded pants from the night before and put them away. He couldn't risk removing the rocks or cleaning them, so this way he could wear them again next weekend. Now he simply needed to figure out how to distribute the rocks discretely before then.

As a history teacher, Trenton knew more than a few odd facts. He knew that in ancient Japan, disgraced warriors would commit "Seppuku," ritual suicide where they cut out their own bowels. He knew that the last name of the man who invented the flushing toilet was Crapper. Yes Crapper. He'd also heard that in order to get rid of unwanted rocks or the like, a prisoner might cut holes in his pockets and let the debris fall right out of the bottom of his pants. Trent thought it a shame to waste of a pair of pants, especially if you we're a prisoner with only two sets of clothes to your name. But he also thought it could be rather helpful in his current situation. Now he just needed to figure out how to do it without getting caught…

■■

The next weekend Trenton woke feeling better than he had in weeks. He put on the pants with the rocks in the pocket. Then he made a quick breakfast for himself, pocketing a knife halfway through. After finishing breakfast he went to the bathroom. While peeing he casually put a hand in the pocket containing the rocks and the knife and poked a hole in the upper part of the pocket, towards his inner thigh, careful to make it small enough that the rest of the rocks were able to rest easily in the bottom of the pocket[1].

Keeping his hands in his pockets, Trenton walked outside; the brisk morning air greeted him and he shivered slightly, his blue t-shirt scant protection from the autumn breeze. Soon enough he'd have to start wearing a jacket.

Trenton continued down the street, approaching the first PTS station on his route. The leaves of the trees he passed were a motley of red, green and yellow, yet there was not a single leaf on the ground. He felt in his pocket for the rocks, surprised by how small they were. His pocket was only about half full but each rock felt no bigger than the tip of a ballpoint pen. All in all, he estimated there were at least twenty of them.

The stairway down to the station was now only a few feet away. The people milling around paid him no attention, but that didn't mean much. Trenton pinched a ball from his pocket and popped it through the hole in the upper portion of his pocket. He felt it slide down his leg, and then it rolled away, becoming just another part of the city. Thankfully these were loose-fitting pants so the pebbles could slide freely down his leg and escape with only minimal difficulty.

Trenton was careful to walk at a measured pace, and even stopped a few times to sit on a conveniently placed bench. He passed seven more PTS stations and each time dropped a pebble nearby. He slowly meandered his way towards the Screens, not exactly looking forward to the sensory overload that awaited him there.

Eventually he forced himself to enter the square. Since he had more than enough pebbles left, and the square was much larger than a PTS station, he decided to place one near each corner of the plaza. He did his best to act as if he was simply inspecting the different Screens.

The rest of the walk proceeded much like these initial stops with Trenton continuing to drop rocks at prime locations for the next 1.01 hours before returning home. He made every effort to ensure that the walk did not appear any different compared to any of his previous strolls.

When he got home, he paid attention to the news for the first time in years. But, like always, it turned out be a waste of time. The newscasters, with their over-enthusiastic voices and plastered smiles,

---

[1] And careful to avoid poking anything else that was nearby.

merely droned on about various people who had recently experienced "noteworthy" things in their lives. And of course they were able to show each and every such event in intimate detail. Trenton knew he shouldn't be surprised. Even if something had happened to take out some of the cameras, the government would never admit to it publicly, or even permit a hint of the news to spread.

So Trenton resigned himself to waiting until he could return to The Black Cat with the hopes of running into someone with more information. When the weekend finally came, Trent rushed[1] to the bar, desperate to learn what had happened.

He sat and ordered a drink, looking around for the man – Cleft – who had given him the job in the first place. Seeing no one he recognized, he deflated a little in his seat. He took a great gulp of beer and glared sullenly at the bartender for a second before pulling himself together.

"Long week?" a woman asked from her seat two stools down, her brown eyes examining Trenton's childlike display with amusement. Her legs rested on the bottom rung of her chair, only partially covered by the hem of a dark blue dress.

"Yep. Just like most weeks," Trenton replied, but his expression lightened a hair.

"At least you don't have a terminal disease slowly eating you from the inside out," the girl said, eyeing him.

"Uh… do you?" Trenton debated scooting farther away, but decided that even if she was contagious, he might not mind getting infected.

The woman laughed. "Nope. Just trying to make you feel better."

Trenton smiled back. "Well it did take my mind off of everything else. I was half worried I'd have to grab a human shield if you were contagious."

"Well in honor of neither of us being on the edge of death, let's have another round." She gestured to the bartender and two more beers clanked down in front of them.

The two talked for a couple more hours, only getting moderately drunk, when the woman said, "I know this club on the other side of town. It's a bit more exciting than this place if you want to come."

[1] If you could even call it that. It was a fast-paced walk.

Trenton knew this girl must be too good to be true, but he also knew that if she somehow *was* this good, he'd be the biggest idiot in the world to say no. Anyway, it was only 9:58, too early to head home, and he clearly wasn't going to learn anything useful tonight.

"Sure, sounds fun." He got up from his stool.

The girl (her friends call her Betty) led him out of the bar. They made their way to the nearest PTS station, encountering only the occasional stray wanderer on the way. They descended the steps and Trenton stepped forward to call a Pod when the girl pulled him back.

"Hold on a minute." She guided Trenton over to the side of the station. Drawing closer to him, she whispered in his ear. "The 'rocks' you scattered messed with any nearby devices that link to your ring. That link is what allows the government to capture footage of everything. Your ring doesn't store any audio or visuals, just sends them right on through the link. The signal can't reach underground by itself so it needs those devices to receive information from the rings. The 'rocks' permanently modified those devices so that we can turn them on and off at will. The cameras down here go through the same devices so those can't get through to The Program either.

"So, basically, the government can't see or hear anything we say down here if you don't want them to?"

"Mhm. You're having a completely private conversation for the first time since the beginning of The Program."

Trenton shook his head. "I find it hard to believe they won't figure out something is wrong."

"They will eventually. But the beauty of it is that they're focusing all their attention on fixing everything near the Screens, since it's such a public spectacle. And we let the devices transmit to The Program except when we want to talk in private, which makes it much less obvious that anything is wrong."

Trenton tried to process everything that Betty had told him (it was a pretty dense speech, I know). What he couldn't get beyond though, was how these people had managed to obtain this information. "How exactly do you know all of this? No one except for the government itself has access to this information."

She gave him a pointed look. "You really think no one else would have found a way into the government's network? No matter how advanced the network becomes, there will always be someone able to hack into it. The other reason I brought you down here was to tell you about a meeting that's going to be down here in about a month.

"But we've already spent too long here. Let's go." And with that she took Trenton's hand, ending his first private conversation in twenty years.

CHAPTER NINE

Trenton continued going to the bar every other weekend but heard nothing more from the Resistance. He heard some talk of work being done on the Screens, but besides that, he had no idea if the government had even discovered the faulty equipment in the PTS stations yet.

The first snow hit 25 days, 3 hours, and 41 minutes after the end of Trenton's stroll with the rocks. The snow brought ever-shorter days and the all too familiar chill of winter. People went about their lives, venturing out into the open air only with a specific destination in mind, and a bundle of clothes wrapped tightly around their bodies.

For the most part, Trenton was no different, only walking to and from work during the week. He still occasionally walked the city when the weekend came around, just with a few more layers than usual. Some people fought longer than others, but soon any memory of warm sunlight on bare skin was completely forgotten, as the world transformed from the gray of concrete and metal to that of month-old snow and slush.

Relief came with the realization that the meeting in the PTS station that Betty had told him about was finally happening tonight.

He arrived at the station at exactly 10:11 pm (the predetermined time was 10:12). When he stepped out of his Pod, he was surprised by how ordinary the station appeared. There were a few people scattered about; no one seemed sure of what they should do. They barely looked up as Trenton went to stand by one of the white tiled walls.

A second later, a somewhat stout man with a full black beard coughed loudly and the three other people in the room quickly hushed and drew closer to him. The man said quietly, "The odds of someone walking into this particular station at this time of night, in the middle of winter are small, but we can't take any chances. We have five minutes for this meeting. We'll know if anyone comes near the stairs or is arriving in a Pod, since we hacked into the cameras surrounding the street entrance and are monitoring the incoming railways. If I say to leave, we break apart and go our separate ways without another word.

"Now, to start with, let's congratulate this man on his work some months ago," the man continued, pointing at Trenton. "Because of him we were able to get a lot done, not the least of which was rigging this station to work only when we want it to. You're all relatively new members so I'll give you some basic information as fast as I can.

"First, we don't share our real names. This won't stop a mole, or someone being tortured by the government from identifying faces, but it at least makes it harder for them to obtain our true identities. For the same reason, we each interact with only a few other members and only rarely do we work with the same person repeatedly. And third, our goal is to end The Program and anything related to it, by any means necessary."

They all nodded in understanding.

"Now that that's out of the way, I'll speak with each of you individually. Let's spread out in case someone walks in."

The man talked to a young woman first, and after a minute she left the station. Next the man walked over to Trenton and handed him a coin. "This is your reward for the work you did."

"A quarter? I feel honored. Except these are worthless – the city hasn't used coins since the '20s." Trenton felt a twinge of anger. He hadn't expected any reward, but he didn't appreciate being mocked.

"It's not for you to spend," the man said, ignoring Trenton's tone. "That quarter is like those rocks you used, except it only turns on when in contact with bare skin. It'll block communications to any rings within ten feet for the first ten seconds, and then it expands to temporarily knock out any cameras and rings within a hundred feet.

In that first stage, it's pretty unlikely to be noticed, so it's very useful for a quick private word to someone. But if you hold it for more than ten seconds, someone will know something's wrong. They might not connect it to you the first time, but after the second time, you can be sure they will."

"So basically if I don't want to be tortured on TV, I *shouldn't* use it full-out twice," Trenton said.

"Exactly. Use it, don't abuse it."

"Like drugs."

The man just stared at him, and moved on to the next person.

"Guess that means it's my turn to leave," Trenton said to himself.

■■

Trenton stopped at a bar near the PTS station where the meeting had been held for a few drinks before he returned home, worn out. He mechanically went about his nighttime routine, and by 12:40 was in bed, ready for sleep.

He woke late the next morning, panicked for a moment, then remembered it was Saturday. He made a light breakfast for himself, and turned on a holographic display using his ring. There wasn't much of interest on at this hour, so he watched the news as he ate.

All too quickly, a trial came on. Trenton grimaced and moved to change the channel, when he froze.

He took in the man's sand-colored hair, the cleft chin –

and knew for sure. It was Cleft.

Trying to keep his face from betraying him, he lowered his hand. Before he changed the channel he had to at least learn the man's real name. They very rarely released names of the victims but maybe this would be one of those times. The announcer was going on about how Cleft was a member of the Resistance and had attempted (unsuccessfully, they claimed) to sabotage The Program.

Cleft sat calmly in the metal chair, his hands and ankles bound tightly. Trenton was unsure if he should be worried for his own safety. He had been at the bar with him that night – had gotten his orders from him; it felt like ages ago.

They would investigate those close to him, as well as any suspicious activity, but Trenton had only seen the man once and he figured if they had found any connection, they would have brought him in by now.

The TV panned to show the two men walking in with their heavy briefcases. Trenton kept waiting for them to flash his name on the screen, or for the announcer to say it in passing. He waited while they chopped off a foot. While they burned his hand black. Trenton waited till they set fire to his entire body. The man flailed, still strapped in the chair, as his body burned like a torch.

Trenton waited.
But he died. Nameless.

CHAPTER TEN

Trenton sat in a stupor, the light from the H-Display washing over him. Over the course of the day he had moved maybe fifteen feet in total. Once to transition to the living room and once to relieve himself. He sat in the otherwise dark room, staring at the pictures on the screen, hearing the chatter of voices, but registering neither.

He knew he should get up, walk around, eat dinner, do *something*. But he couldn't remember why he should do these things. So he did nothing.

Eventually he pulled himself to bed and fell into a restless sleep. The first half of the next day followed a similar pattern. This would have continued on until Trenton was forced to work, but mercifully, his ring beeped at 1:03 pm, alerting him to an incoming call: his sister Jessica.

"Hey, you doing anything?" Her voice rang out of the closest speaker in the room, far too chipper for Trenton's liking.

"I'm kind of feeling a laid-back day, Jess," he said, hoping she would get the hint.

"We can just get a late brunch. That's pretty laid back."

Trenton didn't respond, but his stomach rumbled.

"Come on, Sunday's our day Trent!" Jessica added.

"We don't have a day. But fine. Where are we eating?"

"That place down on 4th. Suzanne's or whatever. Be there in ten."

"No I need to shower," he said, realizing how disheveled he must look. "Make it twenty. See you." He tapped his ring to hang up.

Exactly 20 minutes and 30 seconds later, Trenton walked into the diner. His sister was of course nowhere to be found. Another five minutes passed before she finally came through the door.

"Good thing I rushed over here," Trenton grouched as they sat down at a table.

"Oh shush. A couple minutes never killed anyone."

"That's just not true. I'm sure plenty of people have died because something arrived just a few minutes late," Trenton said.

Jess just looked at him. "You look like shit."

"I just showered."

"You don't look dirty, you look shitty. There's a difference." She smirked at him. "But seriously, are you okay?"

Trenton was quiet for a moment, debating how to respond. "I'm just wondering what the point of all this is."

"What? Life?" Jess asked.

"Yeah."

"There is no point, you idiot, " she said smiling a little. And somehow, Trenton actually felt better, if only for 37 minutes.

∎∎

The next week went by painfully slow. During the day, Trenton struggled to keep it together, and at night his dreams were mildly disturbing: sometimes he was the one being tortured while other times he was the one holding the knife, holding the blowtorch, laughing as his unnamed victim burned.

He started sleeping less and less but continued to lay in bed during the hours he normally slept, not wanting to alert the cameras to his inexplicably fragile state. By Thursday, he feared he was losing his mind. By Friday, he was sure of it. It was in the final few minutes of class on Friday when it happened. He had begun to relax, knowing the weekend would bring some relief, and so was caught off guard when a student asked, "Why does the government televise their trials? Is there some historical reason?"

Trenton visibly shuddered and was unable to respond. Twenty-one pairs of eyes and the dark lens of a camera stared at him. Silence descended. Silence so thick a butter knife would be useless. You'd need at least a steak knife, but maybe even that wouldn't do the trick.

The bell rang, ending the moment that had felt like an hour. Trenton was sure now that they would come for him. That question had been planted to mess with his head, to get him to confirm his guilt. But he'd keep his poker face until he was accused of treason during his own (most likely public) trial. He held on to the shredded remains of his sanity, hoping that he was wrong.

The students trickled out of the room, leaving Trenton standing there. After another moment, he forced himself into action. He turned off the board at the front of the class, turned off the lights, and left the room. He walked through the hallways, imagining a government official around every corner. The cold air shocked him out of his paranoia (mostly) and Trenton figured he had at least a few more days of freedom, since they hadn't accosted him yet.

While sitting in a Pod on his way home, Trenton had a thought that failed to lighten his mood at all: the weekend was here.

∎∎

Jason called on Saturday. Trent was outside enduring the cold, preferring physical discomfort to an empty house with far too few distractions. He was wearing gloves, a thick brown jacket, and a hat, but he was by no means warm. When Trenton tapped his ring through his glove to answer the call, he was surprised by how normal his voice sounded. The last time they had spoken had been the day he had slipped him the note that had eventually catapulted Trenton into the thick of the Resistance.

"Hey Jason." He brought the hand with the ring up to his ear because the wind was making it difficult to hear, even with the ring's advanced microphone and speaker.

"Trent, you up for a little get-together tonight? I was thinking just you, me, and a few other people."

"Uh, sure why not," Trenton said, trying to sound excited. He sounded more like he was agreeing to a colonoscopy.

"Ok, be at my place at seven." The call terminated and Trenton was left out in the cold, wondering what exactly this "get-together" would consist of.

He spent the rest of the afternoon back indoors, having faced all the cold he could handle for one day. On the way back to his apartment he had told his ring to turn the heat up, so that by the time he stepped through the door, he was met with a wonderful wave of warm air. A few minutes later he was on the couch with a cup of microwaved hot-chocolate, prepared to hibernate for the next 5.3 hours until he had to meet up with Jason.

When the time finally came to venture back outdoors, he slowly got up from the couch and re-bundled himself in his substantial outdoor attire. At 6:59, he knocked on Jason's door. Eleven seconds later, the door opened and Trent was ushered inside. Whereas Trenton and many others owned or rented apartments, Jason lived in a quieter part of the city and owned his own small house. As a result, he had quite a bit more space. The rooms were more open, with high ceilings and few separating walls, leaving the impression that the house went on forever. It was perfect for parties; unlike most of their houses, more than two people could have a conversation at a time and no one got squished. In fact, they'd had a party there over the past summer. That was probably the last time Trenton had been to the house. Jason led Trenton into a dimly lit room with a black upright piano in one corner.

Jason handed Trent a drink and gestured for him to sit. "You're the first one here. Everyone else is fashionably late – the bastards," he joked.

"I figured that would happen but I didn't care enough to sit at home waiting," Trent replied.

Jason laughed and sat down on the chair opposite him.

"So what exactly is the plan for tonight?" Trenton asked.

"I figured we'd go to a few bars or just get something to eat. Plus, there's someone coming I think you'll like."

"Don't tell me this is a double date. You're just trying to find me a girl so you and Emily will have another couple to hang out with," Trent said. "Is there anyone else even coming besides this random girl and your wife, Emily?"

"Nope. But this girl really is great, Trent. She's smart, beautiful, and just as sarcastic as you are."

"Well, it's not like I can say no now anyways." As Trent finished speaking they heard the door open and 37 seconds later two women walked into the room.

The blond, who Trenton recognized as Emily, said, "Hey guys, sorry we're late. Trent, this is Molly."

Trent half-lifted a hand from his knee in greeting. Molly smiled in response and Trenton took a third of a moment to compose himself. Her reddish-brown hair was closer to straight than curly, her skin a shade darker than pale.

Belatedly, Trenton decided to stand. "It's nice to meet you." He misjudged how close she was to the front of his chair, and mentally (as well as physically) flailed as he rose from his seat in order to avoid touching her, almost falling right back down in the process.

After he had regained his mental (and physical) composure, she stepped back, giving him an amused look. "It's nice to meet you as well. These two have been telling me about you for what seems like forever."

"I hope they didn't tell you *everything*, because that would just ruin the aura of mystery I cloud myself in. It's my only asset really."

"So the only good thing about you is what nobody knows? Maybe you shouldn't tell people that," she said, laughing.

Jason looked at the H-Display in the corner of the room, checking the time, and said, "He's selling himself short, Molly. We'll let him tell you the truth at dinner, where we should really be heading to now."

They made their way to dinner, keeping up a steady stream of small talk. It had been long enough that Trenton could barely remember how, not that he had ever been particularly good at finding random, unnecessary things to say.

Fortunately, Molly, as well as Jason and Emily kept the conversation rolling, and Trenton added his thoughts whenever they were relevant.

When they arrived at the restaurant, Jason guided them to their table, using his ring. The meal flew by, and Trenton was caught off guard by just how much he was enjoying Molly's company. He learned she was a linguist, and he told her he was a history teacher at the Schools.

By the end of the night Trent was vaguely surprised to discover he wanted to see her again. He was more surprised that she seemed to feel the same. Jason and Emily left them to head home, and the two of them continued to talk, eventually ending up back at the door to her apartment.

"So, I guess this is goodnight," Trenton said.

"You could come in if you want." She looked at him.

He debated for only a second. "No I'd better get home."
Without another word he turned and left, leaving her alone in the
deserted hallway.

CHAPTER ELEVEN

The next morning Trenton woke, cursed himself, and went about his usual routine. At least thoughts of Molly were taking up part of the time he usually spent thinking about the trial. He still felt like he was stuck in the bottom of a deep hole, but the hole was no longer being backfilled, burying him alive. He debated getting Molly's number from Jason, just to try and explain his sudden departure the night before, but held himself back.

Images of Cleft's murder flooded back into his mind, and he wondered just how much the government knew. Were they as ignorant about him as they seemed? Or were they simply biding their time until they could completely break him. He couldn't know for sure and worrying about it would only make his life that much more difficult. So he tried to forget. For now.

The next day, it was time to go back to school. He managed to get through the day without any further incidents. The students who had been present for his sustained silence on Friday acted the same as always and he hoped the incident had gone unnoticed.

On the way back home, he touched the tip of a finger to the coin in his pocket, thinking of all the things he couldn't do. He couldn't tell Molly the truth, couldn't teach what he really believed about The Program, couldn't go a day without thinking of the cameras that constantly monitored him and everyone else in the city.

Then with a jolt, he broke contact with the quarter, remembering what happened after ten seconds. Thankfully, his mind had been moving very quickly and only 7.9 seconds had passed, but he resolved to be more careful with the coin. It could be the difference between ending up on trial and living to fight the government another day.

When Trenton got home, he pulled up a virtual calendar from his ring, checking all the mind-bendingly exciting things he had planned. They consisted of work and sleep. "Damn," Trenton muttered. "I should call her."

He saw that the holidays were fast approaching, along with the longest night of the year. Kids would have a week off, which meant Trenton would too. He wasn't sure whether to be happy or worried about that.

Sighing, he flipped to a search screen and found Jason. He wasn't up for a conversation about his date with Molly so he decided to message him instead. He activated the virtual keyboard with his ring as he sat down in the living room, placing it a few inches above his lap. It had taken him some time to learn to type on a keyboard without any tactile resistance, but like most citizens of the city, Trenton had had more than enough practice. He quickly typed out the message and sent it before he could change his mind.

Less than a minute later he got a response: a link to Molly's ring. Trent could hardly remember the last time they had used actual phone numbers or usernames. Now it was just a matter of getting a link based on the person's full name or address. Or if you were meeting in person, simply agreeing to exchange numbers would automatically add the other person's ring to your contacts. Another benefit of The Program. Trenton almost laughed. Almost.

But enough stalling. Trenton tapped on the link to Molly's ring, adding her to his contacts. Then he tapped on the call button and waited for her to answer. Or to ignore him. Ya nevah knew wat dese cray bitches and hoes would du.

Wow, he really needed to stop watching that Program "The Streets." It was completely ridiculous. No one actually talked like that in the city but people faked those accents just to get viewers tuning in every week.

While these riveting thoughts were flowing through his brain, Molly finally decided to answer his call.

"Hello?"

"Ah, hi Molly, it's Trent."

"I know I just didn't expect you to call after how you stormed off last weekend."

Trenton grimaced. "Yeah, I wanted to apologize about that. I hadn't been on a date in a long time and I guess I was just nervous. I'd love to see you again though."

He could hear her light breathing as she thought it through. "Ok. I'll give you one more chance. Don't fuck it up."

Trenton breathed out a semblance of a laugh as she hung up.

■■

Friday night found Trenton back at The Black Cat. He hadn't been in a few weeks and his date with Molly wasn't till Saturday, so he figured he should make an appearance in the off chance someone from the Resistance was there. He was ordering his second drink when the black-bearded man from the PTS station meeting sat down next to him.

They chatted for a few minutes, then Trenton asked quietly, coin in his hand, "Is there anything I can do?

"Just keep your head down for now. It's going to be a long-ass winter." He didn't say anything else for nearly ten minutes. He just sat with his drink, watching the H-Display in the corner.

Trent had come close to giving up when the man, still looking at the screen, said, "I think this goes without saying, but don't trust anyone. There are more than just cameras watching us."

With that, he got up and walked away. Trenton wondered what had put the man in such a good mood. Maybe he was paranoid now after Cleft's trial. He took another long drink.

After another hour and five minutes at the bar, Trenton decided to call it a night. He returned home, but couldn't fall asleep for what felt like 2.45 hours, his mind fixating on what the man from the bar had said, not that he'd said anything particularly helpful. Trenton had the unsettling feeling that he was missing something. Something important. Eventually he managed to fall asleep, but his dreams were filled with the accusatory faces of family, friends, and complete strangers. They screamed silently at him, yet he had no idea what he had done.

The next day was warm for that time of year, clocking in at 47.2 degrees Fahrenheit. As Trenton went about his day, he stifled the thoughts and feelings from last night, hoping they were just a byproduct of alcohol mixed with the stress of being part of the Resistance.

Soon enough the sun dipped down behind the buildings, leaving the city encompassed by a badly mixed cocktail of darkness and man-made light. Right about this time, Trenton was getting ready. He had just exited the shower and was putting on what he hoped were at least somewhat fashionable clothes. (They weren't.)

He arrived at Molly's apartment at exactly 7:01, one full minute late. She opened the door before he had even come to a full stop.

"I saw you enter the building from my window," she explained as she let him in.

"Gotchya. So my idea, the idea that I love as a history teacher, was dinner and then a movie."

"So you admit that it's been done a few times before," she smiled.

"It's been done since movies first became popular nearly 150 years ago. But I figure if it's worked that long, the odds are it'll work tonight. Plus, it's not the exact same since there aren't any movie theaters left."

"So where are you planning on watching the movie?"

"My place I guess. After an extravagant dinner of course."

She sat down on plush couch that faced a fireplace and an H-Display. "Well I have a better idea. Why don't we eat shitty food while we watch a movie here? That way we won't freeze while walking around."

The one thing Trenton remembered from his past experience dating was that things went a lot easier if you actually listened to the other person. Especially if they might still be angry with you for something, not that Trenton had done anything wrong. Besides basically running away at the end of their last date, that is. "Sure, that sounds great."

They ate popcorn and ordered pizza, and watched a bizarre movie about this man who thought robots were taking over the world, but it was just his imagination.

"I bet it was more because of the acid he must have been doing," Molly snorted, when the "twist" was finally revealed. She was snuggled up next to him under a blanket and Trenton had been keeping as still as possible to avoid ruining it.

Soon after this bombshell of a twist, the credits started to roll. Trenton regretfully disentangled himself and stood to leave.

"Aren't you forgetting something?" Molly asked, standing as well.

"Uhh." Trenton could guess what she meant. He quickly stuck one hand in his pocket to touch the coin, and leaned in. The kiss was as good as could be expected. And by that I mean it was awful. Trenton couldn't even remember the last time he'd kissed someone.

When they broke apart, Trenton did his best to appear nonchalant and said, "I'm a little rusty."

"I gathered that. We'll just have to try again soon." She grinned at him.

Feeling better, he left and made his way home.

■■

The days steadily wore on until the first day of holiday break and then they slowed to a crawl. Jess called, reminding Trenton that he was expected at their old childhood apartment that evening.

"Jess, this is pointless. Forcing us to deal with each other for one night isn't going to fix anything. If anything, it'll make things worse."

"So you're gonna ditch me? Make me eat alone with dad? Thanks a lot, Trent."

He held back a sigh. "No, I'll be there."

"Great! See you at seven!" She hung up.

Trent let loose the sigh. "I can't wait."

At least he'd have more time to see Molly over the next week. They'd only been able to go on a few dates since the movie at her place and they hadn't "taken the plunge" yet, as Jason had so elegantly put it in one of his messages to Trent. But he found himself thinking about her more and more. He just had to make it through tonight first. That would be easy enough if his father had decided he was getting clean again, like he did every-other night. If it weren't his own family, Trenton swore he could have seen some humor in there somewhere.

He halfheartedly got ready, pulling a black button-down shirt over his head and attaching the rest of the buttons. Next came the black dress pants, but no belt. Whenever someone commented on his lack of belt, (which happened more than you might expect) Trenton would claim he didn't own one. He did, he just didn't see the point in wearing a belt when his pants fit fine without it.

After he was ready, he sank back into the couch, enjoying a few minutes of quiet. Then he resigned himself to his fate and started out into the cold, his breath cloudy as it met the frozen air.

When he reached his old home, he stopped for a moment. In the thirteen years, eleven months, and one day since he had left without a backward glance, only returning for the rare holiday dinner, the building had not changed in the slightest. Even the frost on the windows was indistinguishable from that in Trenton's memory.

He entered the building and made his way to the fifth floor. He knocked on his old door and a second later it swung inward, revealing the moderately disheveled figure of Trent's father.

"Come in, come in. Your sister's already here." He held a bottle loosely in one hand, but was steady on his feet as he led Trent inside. The inside had changed even less than the outside. The walls were a plain white, the floor covered in tan tiles with some areas further blanketed with rugs.

They walked from the hallway into the kitchen, where Jessica sat at the counter, doing her best to remain cheerful.

"Hey Trent," she said, glancing at him.

"Hey. The food almost ready?" Jess had taken the liberty of buying the necessary groceries and arriving at the house early to cook; they both knew their father wouldn't be of much help. Trenton felt a stab of guilt.

Jess didn't appear to notice. "Almost. Just a few more minutes in the oven."

When the food was ready, they sat down and Trent watched as Jess made a conscious attempt to keep a conversation going, while his father half-heartedly engaged her. As the meal wore on, brief pauses turned into long silences, and Trent's father continued to pour drinks down his throat.

"Damn your mother."

Really dad, this again? Trent kept himself from saying.

Despite the heavy silence, the (now very drunk) man continued on. "Didn't she know what the hell would happen to her? She didn't think about shit. Left us to be fucked up by seeing what they did to her. And the whole city watching along with us. Then watching us try and survive afterwards. Fuckin' vultures."

Trenton wanted to interrupt, if only to stop the painful memories washing over him, but still couldn't find his voice.

"Who runs away from their family and tries to escape a city that sees everything? As if she'd ever get away."

Jess looked like she was going to be sick so Trent did his best to pacify his father. "You're right. But there's nothing we can do about what happened, so just let it go."

The old man made an indignant noise, but surprisingly did as he was asked. However, this left another hole in the conversation. As the silence grew, Trenton resolved to leave at the first chance he got. He had been there less than an hour, but he felt that given the circumstances, that was more than enough time.

Before he could formulate an excuse, Jess said, "Make sure to save room for dessert. I made chocolate bread pudding."

Trenton's resolve melted away, becoming as soft as the core of the aforementioned pudding. He couldn't leave his sister here. Plus he knew from experience how good the desert would be.

When Jess finally decided it was time, she and Trent cleared the table while their father remained sullenly in his chair. Jess extracted the chocolate bread pudding, and the warm, chocolaty scent caused Trent to salivate.

"Wow Jess, that smells way too good," he said as he carried it over to the table.

"It is." She shot one fifth of a smile at him.

They all dug into the dessert, occupying their mouths so they wouldn't have to search for something to say.

Their father had stopped drinking, so by the end of the dessert, he had managed to pull his head out of his ass. When Jess at long last decided to leave, Trent was right beside her. They were on their way out the door when their father spoke. "I'm sorry. You both deserved better. From your mom and from me."

Trenton guided Jess the rest of the way out of the room and closed the door behind them, leaving the old man standing lost in the hallway of their past.

■■■

They walked with their heads down against the cold night air. Knowing that Jess was upset, Trent had offered to accompany her. The two of them made their way to Jess's apartment, enjoying a silence far more companionable then any from earlier that evening.

When they arrived at her building, Trenton stopped her before she could hurry inside.

"You ok?" he asked, unsure what else to say.

"Yeah I'm fine. I just don't understand our parents. Either one of them."

"Well somehow we're doing ok."

She looked like she wanted to say something, but all that came out was a muted sound that Trenton took as agreement. Then she shot forward and hugged him tightly. Trenton hugged her back. About 4.5 seconds later, she let go, said goodbye, and walked into her building.

Trenton stood there for a second before starting back to his own apartment.

When he stepped into his home, he quickly considered a few options. He could sleep, but that didn't seem very appealing at the moment. He could watch The Program, but he wanted something active and engaging. He activated the game mode on his ring as he slipped on the gloves that would allow his hands to feel tactile feedback from the generated holograms. A screen popped up with various settings and he chose a jungle area with a highly randomized, action-survival setting.

As soon as he touched the last button, the room around him transformed into a lush jungle: the speakers scattered around the room worked in harmony, filling the space with the sounds of crickets, snakes, and rustling leaves. The sun was just about to set, leaving only a dim light that fought to penetrate the thick foliage above him.

Trenton took out the flashlight that had appeared in the belt[1] around his waste. Time moved much quicker in the game world, so he would soon be left entirely in the dark.

He started walking in a random direction, knowing something would happen soon. There was no threat of him walking into a wall; the floor in the middle of the room had been converted at the game's start into a sort of giant treadmill. It anticipated his steps using the multitude of camera's from the ring and was able to match his stride so that he never moved more than a foot or two in any direction.

---

[1] It was a virtual belt of course. We've already gone over Trenton's dislike of belts. Get it together.

Just when he was beginning to question the integrity of the action setting, a voice shouted, "Don't move!" Trenton slowly turned around, hands raised, trying to glimpse the speaker in the near-total darkness. The man came closer and Trent was able to make out a few things of note: the man was bald, wore camouflage clothing, and was pointing an unnecessarily large gun right at Trenton's face.

"Can I help you?" Trent asked.

"Yeah, you can tell me why the hell you're out here." The man didn't lower the gun.

"Just looking for a little adventure."

"This is a dangerous place for that. We're in the middle of a war. For all I know, you could be one of them."

Trent took a chance and said, "Do I really look like I'm fighting on either side? All I have with me is a flashlight. If you just let me go, I'll do my best to stay out of everyone's way."

The man thought it over for a second. "Well you don't seem to be much of a threat. But unless you have a death wish, I'd get the hell out of here."

"Don't worry about me. I'll stay out of sight."

The soldier gestured with his gun, dismissing him, and Trenton jogged quickly away. As he ran through the forest, the remaining light faded away, forcing him to rely solely on his flashlight.

He stopped to rest for a minute when he heard the snap of a branch behind him. He twirled around, casting the beam of light back and forth, but the thick vegetation worked in tandem with the darkness, reducing his visibility to only a few feet. Another crunch and Trenton dropped to the ground as gunfire immediately followed. He snapped off his flashlight and crawled away from the harsh rattle of bullets, hoping he didn't blunder right into something worse.

Luckily, he made it to safety without a snake or like-minded creature ending his (virtual) life prematurely. He stood up and turned his flashlight back on now that the gunfire seemed a "safe" distance away.

What he saw in the beam of light caused his breath to catch in his throat. A fully-grown jaguar crouched on a low-hanging branch less than five feet away. Trent began to slowly back away while keeping his eyes on the oversized cat. The animal tensed, and Trent dove to the side as the jaguar leaped towards him, missing by inches.

Trenton gasped out a breath of relief as the cat continued on instead of returning for another round. Rising shakily to his feet with the help of a nearby shrub, he resumed his retreat away from the cat and the erratic gunfire.

As he made his way through the undergrowth, he began to make out the shapes of plants and small animals without the aid of his flashlight. Even factoring in the accelerated passage of time, the night was still in its nascence. Trenton kept moving, perplexed by the strengthening light and the jumble of cries that sprang up all around him.

Breaking through a layer of foliage, he understood: in front of him were the remnants of a war camp - as well as a quickly spreading fire doing its best to devour anything and anyone it could. The placement and behavior of the fire made it clear that it was chemical in nature.

Trent turned ninety degrees and ran parallel to the fire, hoping to avoid threats to his life, both old and new. To his surprise, he had no difficulty outpacing the fire, and a few minutes later all was dark and silent[1] once more.

He continued walking, sure there was another threat right around the corner. Confirming his suspicions, another soldier appeared from behind a tree, gun balanced in both hands.

The man shifted from one foot to another nervously. "What side are you on?"

"I'm not on a side. I'm just caught in the middle."

"We're fighting a fucking battle and some random guy just happens to be sneaking around? I have a hard time buying that. If I don't shoot you, you might come back at me from behind when I'm fighting. I can't risk it." In the ambient light of the flashlight (which was now pointing at the ground), the man looked near to panicking.

"Look at me. Do I look like a threat?"

"I can't let you go. Can't..."

Trenton took a step forward to try and do something – anything – but the man tensed, his finger tightening around the trigger, and unleashed a round of bullets into Trenton's soft body. Everything went black.

Then the light slowly returned, leaving Trenton in his living room, unharmed but pulsing with adrenaline. A screen came up with the stats from the game. He had lasted 26 minutes and 22 seconds. "It felt a

---

[1] Silent for a jungle – so still pretty damn loud. Just full of sounds that were *supposed* to be there.

lot longer than that." Trenton said as he made his way to the couch, thoroughly exhausted.

He took a quick shower and then flopped down on his bed. Within a minute, he was asleep.

CHAPTER TWELVE

The next day was gray even by normal standards for the city during the winter months. The odds of a heavy snow were high, at least as far as Trenton could tell. Also, he and Molly were supposed to go walking today, so anything that *could* go wrong, probably would.

He tapped his ring and brought up Molly's information, hesitated for a second, then hit the call button.

"Hi Trent! I hope you're not calling to cancel our walk."

"No I just wanted to make sure you'd be okay in the snow. Cause it looks like snow to me."

She laughed. "It looks like snow to you? Did you even check the weather?"

"They're wrong often enough that it's not worth checking."

"Trent, I know you're a history teacher and all, so you're probably stuck in a time where the weather-man was wrong a third of the time," Molly teased. "But the weather reports are more than 90% accurate now. Hold on, I'll check for us."

5.5 seconds later: "Yep you're right, it's definitely going to snow tonight."

"See? I don't need a weather report. So what do you want to do?"

"Let's just bundle up and go anyways. It might end up being even more fun."

Trenton agreed, and tapped his ring to end the call, wondering how he would fill the rest of the day. He decided to go to the gym. It had been weeks since he had even thought of exercising, but today felt like the right day. This was in spite of, or maybe because of, the terrible weather that was coming

There was a public gym only a few blocks from his apartment, so he threw on some shorts and an aging gray t-shirt, and walked over. He wore no jacket or gloves, figuring he could handle the cold for a few minutes (and he didn't want to have to pay the fee for a locker). Needless to say he was shivering by the time he walked through the double doors and into the 73-degree building.

He climbed the stairs to the second floor where the treadmills and lighter weights made their home. Although he had never been a great runner, his all-around fitness was fairly good. After all, he was in his early thirties and exercised semi-regularly (at least that's what he told himself).

However his run found him out of breath quicker than usual and he managed only 3.09 miles at an 8:35 pace before calling it quits. Sweating in the synthetic heat, he rushed back outside, actually enjoying the biting cold for the first 32 seconds. Then his sweat hardened, and his body expelled all it's excess heat, leaving him feeling frozen solid.

He quickened his pace and made it back to his apartment, ready for a hot shower, but when he moved to open his door, he found it already unlocked. Trenton always locked his door. Cautiously, he walked into his apartment. The black shelves looked untouched, the few personal items in their usual place. He glanced at the picture frame that cycled between photos. Nothing wrong there. Finally he conceded defeat; nothing was out of place, but something felt off. Someone must have been here.

He examined the entire house, but nothing was gone, as far as he could see. He absentmindedly put his hands in his pockets and paused. His coin was, of course, in one of his shorts' pockets. Was that what they had been looking for? Did they suspect him of being part of the Resistance? It didn't make sense. The government never thought twice about simply abducting anyone who had even the slightest chance of being involved with the fight against The Program. At least anyone that he knew of.

Jumping in the shower, Trenton did his best to put the search out of his mind. After toweling dry and making himself an egg and bacon sandwich, he felt much better. The calm and satisfaction of a good workout followed by good food always helped him put things into perspective. If the government knew anything, they would have already taken him.

His only option was to keep doing what he had been doing, and wait for a chance to cause serious damage to The Program. He couldn't know what they knew or planned, but as long as he had a chance to fight back, he had to take it.

Later that day, a light snow began to fall, a mere foreshadowing of the storm that loomed. Trenton was busy armoring himself in a thick woolen jacket and black snow pants when his ring dinged. It connected to a nearby speaker and announced in a flat voice, "Molly is at the door."

"Let her in."

Trenton was still struggling with his so-called "armor" when he heard the door open and Molly walked into his room.

"Having a little trouble?" she asked, eyeing his outfit. She, on the other hand, looked perfectly at ease. Her thick coat and snow pants did nothing to diminish her good looks.

"This zipper's just stuck," he said as he continued pulling futilely on the zipper to his snow pants.

"Let me help." She drew closer and before Trenton could argue or realize what was happening, she had zipped his pants all the way up.

"Wow, I'm impressed," Trent said, recovering his wits.

"It just needed a gentle hand. You were trying to brute-force it. That's not usually going to work." She was still standing close to him.

Without thinking, Trenton kissed her and, after a second, she kissed him back, hard. He wrapped his arms around her waist, but their numerous layers of clothes kept their bodies from touching. She wrapped her arms around his head to no greater success.

When they separated for a breath, Molly flashed a mischievous grin. "You know, we could always go for a walk later."

Trent was sorely tempted, but said, "If we wait, we won't even be able to walk without falling over, the snow will be so high."

"You're probably right." She stepped back and they made their final preparations.

Once they were entirely bundled up, they made their way out into the storm. The snow was falling in thick clumps and the sky was dark gray, as what would have been sunset came and went without the slightest acknowledgement. The two figures held on to each other for support against the howling wind, and trudged through the snow.

"So far I'm having less fun than I thought!" Trenton had to yell to Molly from inches away in order to be heard. They had been outside for a full three minutes and zero seconds.

"Oh, don't be a baby! You're the one who wanted to do this in the first place." But she drew even closer to him as the storm continued to grow in strength.

Together they trekked down the street, each step its own battle against the ever-thickening snow. The street was empty, which was the real sign that something was wrong. Even late at night, there was always a stray car or pedestrian wandering the streets. But not today. Today, they were alone in the city.

Trenton could barely see his hand in front of his face – couldn't hear anything besides the whip of the wind. Unable to hold back, he let loose a roaring laugh. A laugh that no one in the entire city could hear, not even Trenton himself. Molly looked over at him, and her eyes, the only part of her left uncovered, seemed to laugh along with him.

They stayed on the sidewalks, unnecessarily[1] wary of the lasers that covered the roads, heating up and melting the bottom layer of the snow so it could drain into the Water Disposal and Recycling System. By morning the roads would be completely clear, the only reminder of the previous night the snow piled on the sidewalks, and even that would be disposed of soon enough.

The cold started to seep through Trenton's defenses and he could feel Molly start to tremble next to him.

He leaned close to yell in her ear. "Okay, I can feel you shivering. I think that means its time to go back."

At first, it looked liked she wanted to keep going, but she didn't resist when Trenton turned them around and started back. He raised the hand wearing the ring and yelled at it, "Turn up the heat to eighty degrees for when we get back!"

Molly started to falter so Trent let her lean on him, half dragging her the rest of the way to his building.

Stepping inside the lobby brought a certain level of relief: there was no longer biting wind tearing at them or snow doing its very best to suffocate them. They took the elevator up to the room; neither one of them wanted to face the stairs. At long last, they reached Trent's apartment, throwing open the door to meet the welcomed blast of hot air that greeted them.

---

[1] Unnecessary because the cameras watching them would shut off any lasers in their or any other persons path.

Inside, they stripped off their now soaking clothes (all four layers) and changed into a fresh set, with Trent giving Molly the privacy of his room. She came out wearing one of his t-shirts and a pair of his jeans. Trenton couldn't help but stare, and she had to remind him that it was his turn to change. After he emerged, feeling much better in fresh, dry clothes, they huddled on the couch for more warmth. Molly's shivering was becoming less and less frequent, and Trent was feeling warm for the first time in what felt like a year.

"You okay?" Trent asked.

"Yeah, I think so. Almost warm now. I don't know if I would have made it back without you."

"You probably wouldn't have been out there in the first place, either."

"True. But still, thanks." She smiled at him.

In that moment, everything that had occurred over the last few months seemed incredibly far away. It was hard to believe that not too long ago, he had dreaded facing each day, and each night had been haunted by nightmares of the trials. He had been obsessed with fighting The Program, but had no real hope of making a difference. He hadn't cared about anything else all that much. Now he was still obsessed, but it wasn't the only important thing in his life. It gave him a sense of balance that he had desperately needed but hadn't even considered until now.

Trent wondered if he was being selfish. If Molly wasn't part of the Resistance (which he still wasn't sure about), then he was putting her in danger. If he were discovered, she might be the first to suffer. He had to find out if she was with the Resistance, although he wasn't sure he was strong enough to let her go if he had to.

Molly broke into his thoughts with a light kiss on his cheek. "What are you thinking so deeply about?"

Trenton decided to answer with a version of the truth. "You." By this time, she had stopped shivering and Trenton was actually on the verge of breaking a sweat. "Do you mind if I turn the heat back down? I'm getting hot."

"Sure. I'm warm now too."

Trenton tapped his thumb twice against his ring, which was in its usual place on his pointer finger. "Turn the heat down to 72 degrees." The ring dinged in acknowledgement, and the room reached the stated temperature within minutes.

He looked over at her. "So are we in agreement? That what we just did was really dumb, but I'm happy we did it?"

"That's exactly how I feel. It was amazing! And stupid. But the amazing part made it worth it."

Neither one of them mentioned just what had been so special about being out in the storm. They knew better than that. But they also knew they had shared an experience not many people in the city would ever have the chance to know.

The warmth of Molly's body was close. The only thing between his arm and her skin was the thin material of his borrowed t-shirt. She was curled up, pressed against him with her face angled towards his. He kissed her for the second time that night, and when she started peeling off her clothes, any remaining shreds of his resolve gave out. They spent the rest of the night together.

CHAPTER THIRTEEN

The next morning Trenton awoke with Molly's bare back pressed up against his chest, his arm around her. After enjoying lying in bed for a couple more minutes, he carefully extricated himself, put on some clothes, and walked to the kitchen. He wasn't sure if he should make breakfast. Would that be weird? He wasn't sure, but he *was* hungry and the odds were good Molly would be too.

He made a breakfast of eggs and bacon – the only breakfast worth making – and soon enough Molly walked in, wearing only his t-shirt from last night.

"Mmm, I'm starving." She sat down at the small table in the corner.

Trenton brought the food over; he had made both sunny-side up and scrambled eggs as well as a copious amount of bacon. "Do you want toast or anything else?"

"This looks great the way it is," she said, giving his hand a squeeze from across the table.

They ate in comfortable silence, and afterwards Trenton asked if she had any plans for the day. As it was holiday break and neither of them had anything scheduled, they relaxed at Trent's apartment for the rest of the day.

Trenton only once thought about the Resistance that day, and even that thought centered around Molly. He resolved to get Jason alone and use his coin to ask him if Molly was part of the Resistance. Jason had to know, since he was the one who introduced them.

23 hours and 41 minutes after Molly had first arrived at Trent's apartment, she left the same way she had come in: bundled in layers and layers of clothing (this time still warm from the dryer).

It was Monday evening, but Trent hadn't been to the bar in weeks, and it was a holiday, so he stopped by for a drink. He soon grew bored and sent a message to Jason to see when he could talk.

A response came surprisingly quickly and Trenton wondered if Jason was as bored as he was. It read: *How about in an hour, my place?*

Trenton tapped a quick reply on the virtual keyboard he had set up on top of the bar, confirming it.

That finished, he got up and prepared to face the below-freezing temperatures that awaited him outside. It was as cold as expected on his march back to the apartment. The change in the city in the 27 hours and 15 minutes since his walk in the storm was remarkable. The snow in the streets had long ago melted away and the sidewalks, which had been shoveled by the city's workers, were filled with people. People who watched and were watched, and Trenton was no different.

■■■

Trenton sat in a leather armchair across from Jason, an H-Display blaring in the background. They had been exchanging pleasantries for the last half-hour, and Trenton figured now was as a good a time as ever to bring up Molly.

He grabbed hold of the coin in his pocket, and said quietly, "Ok, we can talk freely for a little if we keep our voices down. I have something that blocks out any device trying to listen in on us."

"Are you sure? How do you know?"

"As sure as I can be. It hasn't failed me so far. And if it doesn't work, screw it. You have to take some risks sometimes." Trenton let go and then regained contact with the coin, remembering that after ten seconds of continual usage it would expand its range from ten to a hundred feet. He got to the point. "Is Molly part of the Resistance? I need to know so I can decide what to do."

"How would I know?"

"What do you mean how would you know? You're part of the Resistance and you introduced me to her, so I thought you would at least have some idea."

"Trent, I got your note, but I'm not part of the Resistance. I thought you would have realized that when no one contacted you." He saw Trenton's expression change. "But someone has contacted you... Shit."

"What does that mean? Who contacted me?"

"Well it could be the Resistance since I'm guessing they have a certain level of access to the government's network. They could have found out somehow that you wanted to be part of it. But if it's not them..."

"If it's not them then who? The government?"

"Yeah it could be them. Or maybe it's someone else we don't even know exists. There's no way to know."

Trenton took a deep breath, re-clasped the coin in his pocket for the fifth time during their conversation, and looked at his friend. "Well I guess I should hope I've been dealing with the Resistance all this time. But if the Resistance somehow figured out how I felt about The Program, wouldn't the government have also?"

"There's a good chance of that. But it's possible that the Resistance was paying closer attention to you, or maybe they're just better at reading subtle signs."

"So there's a small chance I'm not fucked, but I'm pretty much fucked."

"Yep."

"Then get me a beer. Might as well drink while I can."

Jason brought out a chilled six-pack and they spent the rest of the night reminiscing about old friends and old jokes, ignoring the potential doom that lay over their heads.

One week later, Trenton found himself back at work, back at his routine. He still had no idea what to do about Molly. He could be putting her in serious danger and there was always the possibility, no matter how minute, that she was a spy.

Even though he knew all this, he couldn't bring himself to end it. Instead he continued on, acting as if nothing had changed. Nothing was wrong. All the while knowing that sooner or later their time would run out.

When he got home that evening, he sat watching The Program until he went to bed. He slept surprisingly well that night, as he had every night for the last week.

When Friday night rolled around, Trenton headed to the bar on the small chance of finding some answers. Inside, it seemed to be even more hectic than usual, with loud chatter buzzing all around him as Trent moved to his favorite spot at the bar.

He ordered a whiskey and feigned interest in the game being played on the H-Displays. A man sat down next to him and ordered a whisky as well. He had no defining features whatsoever: his hair was brown, skin neither pale nor tan. His face seemed to disappear from your brain the moment your eyes left it. "We've been wondering when you'd be back."

"And who exactly is 'we'?" Trenton asked, irritated.

"Look." The man cradled a coin in his hand, an exact replica of the one in Trenton's pocket, keeping it below the bar so that only Trent could see. "If you keep your voice down, you can say whatever the hell you want. So why don't you tell me who you think we are."

"I *thought* you were the Resistance, but now I'm not so sure."

The man shifted on his stool. "And why's that?"

"Because I just found out that the only person I told about wanting to join the Resistance isn't a part of it and never told anyone anything. So I'm wondering who you are and how you knew about me."

"Your friend dumped your note in the trash. You're lucky we got to it first."

"Shit. He didn't even burn it?"

"Nope. Must've panicked. Understandably. If he'd been caught with that note things would have gone downhill fast."

Trenton grimaced. "Okay, but you didn't answer my first question. Who the hell are you? How would the Resistance, filled with people like me, get access to all that information and advanced technology?"

"That's just it. We're not like you. Our leaders weren't born here. They came from outside. "

"Uh, outside? How? And why?"

"It took us more than ten years since The Program started to get here and almost another ten to make any real progress. Let's just say that. There's not enough time to explain our whole history, but just know we're doing our best to end The Program and the government along with it.

"Just know we're doing our best to help you get free. Right now we need to know if you're still with us. "

Trenton had no idea what motivated these people, but there wasn't much of a choice here. Whether he continued helping them or not, they would still fight the government with their chances only slightly diminished, if at all. If they lost, the people of the city would never know what it was like to walk down the street, to drink a beer, watch a movie, or even sleep, without someone watching.

But if they won, the people of the city were putting their lives in the hands of an unknown entity, an outside force that may be even more terrible than what they currently faced. Trenton could barely guess at what lurked outside the city's limits. What could possibly be the motivation, the end goal, for this group of outsiders suddenly coming to the city's aid?

So Trenton hesitated, but only for a moment. "I'm still with you. But I deserve to know the full story. And sooner would be better than later."

"Come to our PTS station two weeks from today at 8:31pm and we'll tell you more. But for now, you'd better go."

Trenton walked out of the bar.

■■

"Is there a reason you're so quiet, or are you just moping?" Molly asked teasingly.

Trent looked up from the mash potatoes he was playing with. "I've just got a lot to think about." They were sitting in Trent's apartment eating a dinner they had just prepared together.

"Like which kids are getting detention on Monday? Or something more serious." She took a sip of her beer, eyeing him over the top of the glass. "Something's going on. You've been acting weird for days now. Did I do something wrong or what?"

"You didn't do anything."

"Then what is it?"

Trent was silent for 4 seconds.

"Come on, Trent, talk to me."

"I don't want to lie to you."

"Then tell me the truth. It shouldn't be that hard."

"Ok, fine." He pulled the coin out his pocket and said, "this coin, it lets us talk with no one else hearing or seeing us."

Molly didn't look convinced. "Really. And how did you come by such a coin?"

"I'm part of… well part of a resistance against the government. They gave it to me."

"Trent you know you could die for a joke like that."

"It's not a joke."

His calm assuredness slowly convinced her. He put the coin away so that when he broke contact every couple seconds, the cameras wouldn't see anything out of the ordinary. Molly remained silent.

"I'm sorry I didn't tell you sooner. And I'm sorry I've been putting you in danger all this time." She still said nothing. "I understand if this means it's over," he said, praying it wasn't.

Finally she said quietly, "We could both be dead right now, or locked up, or on trial."

"But we're not. And if they haven't found anything out yet, maybe they never will. I'm not asking you to join the Resistance; I'm just asking if you can accept me being a part of it."

"I – I don't know. I need some time to think." She stood and was out the door before Trenton could blink.

Trenton grimaced. *Well that could have gone worse. Maybe. If I had pulled out a gun or something.*

He finished eating, returning to the silence that had filled the room not five minutes prior.

CHAPTER FOURTEEN

"Death is a luxury. It ends miserable lives, sparing further pain and suffering. We rarely kill. Death would be a reward, and there are too few who deserve such a prize. No. We bring you as close to death as we can, cause as much agony as we can – but then we save you. Save you from the relief death brings. So that you may live as an example of what happens to those who betray The Program."

-Director of The Program, video shown exclusively to those put on Trial

Trenton turned off the H-Display, unable to watch another second of The Program. He rolled out of bed, masking his disgust as best as he could. He had been watching TV the night before and must have never turned it off. Dressing quickly, he ran through the issues on the forefront of his mind. First on the list was Molly. Then came the Resistance and, in last place, his mother.

Since Molly was first on the list, he might as well start with her. A week had passed since their conversation, and he hadn't heard from her since. He hadn't tried to contact her, thinking she would reach out to him when she was ready, but he was beginning to wonder if she would ever call. On one level, he completely understood her fears, but another part of him was astounded that anyone would choose to turn their back on a (potentially) great relationship rather than face those fears.

He skipped right over the Resistance, since he hadn't learned anything new about how it had survived and gotten so powerful. Reluctantly, he turned his thoughts to his mother while he made a quick breakfast. However, when he sat down to eat, he found he'd lost most of his appetite.

After shoveling down as much food as he was able (bacon and eggs of course), he threw on a heavy jacket and was on his way. Walking the 19 blocks to his destination, Trent passed the usual towering steel and glass buildings that filled most of the city, accompanied by the perfectly groomed gardens and parks. But the farther he walked, the more his surroundings began to change: buildings shortened and parks became sparse. The one constant was the subtle absence of trash or disorder of any kind. Trenton made his way purposefully through the backside of the city, having made this exact walk sixteen times in as many years.

He entered a particularly squat building that, from the outside at least, had no other distinguishing features from the other buildings surrounding it. Once he stepped inside though, he was confronted with some very subtle signs that this wasn't a typical building: guards were scattered around, with one man sitting at a desk signing in visitors. Behind him was a clear wall that stretched across the entire floor, separating the lobby from a room containing women of all ages, all dressed in orange. So subtle.

Trent joined the line in front of the desk, unconsciously tapping his fingers against his leg as he waited. When the person in front of him had finished, he approached the desk and signed in with his ring. Once the information had gone through, the guard confirmed the reason for his visit, asking him his name and who he was here to see.

"Abigail Trenton," Trenton responded.

"Relation?"

"Mother."

The guard entered some extra information using a virtual keyboard, too quickly for Trenton to follow. "Alright. Go ahead."

Trenton walked up to the clear wall, aiming for the door outlined in a blue light. He'd been told the door would only open if the cameras throughout and around the entire building deemed there was no potential threat. Of course he had to be cleared for entry, but he had a hard time believing anyone would be dumb enough to try to get past the guards without proper consent.

As he passed through the doorway, he saw her. Her black hair was lined with gray, her narrow frame barely more substantial than a whisper.   She was seated at a corner table, and when she saw him look over, she gave a small wave.

He sat down across from her and said, "Hey mom. How are you?"

"Hello Alex. I'm okay. As okay as someone can be when they've been stuck in here for the last seventeen years." A shadow flitted across her face. "How was the holiday dinner with your father and sister?"

"Really great as always," he said, the sarcasm plain in his voice. Trenton reflected on that night from a few weeks back, and found it only moderately painful to do so. "Dad started out the night pretty sober, and ended it that way. But the middle was a little rough."

"What did he do this time? Probably went on about me for a while."

"Yeah. The same old thing about how you left us and destroyed our lives etcetera etcetera."

"You'd think after this long he'd have at least added a new twist or something. Really. It gets boring hearing the same old story of how I ran away for no reason. Next time tell him to throw something more interesting. Like a few murders or something." She forced a smile.

Trenton looked her in the eyes. "But really, why'd you try and leave like that? Were you just afraid of The Program, or was it dad's drinking? I never asked, because I could guess at most of it, but I just don't get why you would leave us and try something so... so senseless."

She let out a deep breath. "I was afraid. And I was selfish. And I was ignorant of just how impossible it really was. Your dad definitely didn't help, but it was my problem. It was my fault."

When Trenton didn't respond, she lowered her eyes, regret plainly visible in her face. "I know it was stupid. I've had the last seventeen years to think about how stupid it was. Even if I had brought you both with me, we would have been more likely to get caught, and you'd be even worse off. I didn't want to risk you both, but I had to do something. I felt like I was suffocating."

Seeing how much pain she was feeling, Trenton decided his mother had suffered enough. Thinking up a less poignant subject, he said, "So... what've you been up to in here the last twelve months?"

"I'm still learning French. I can sort of hold a conversation now, if the other person speaks slowly enough."

"That's great."

They spent the rest of their time avoiding any sensitive topics. After another 21 minutes and 20 seconds, the guards signaled for the visitors to leave, and Trenton found himself walking back to his apartment, unsure of what he was feeling.

He tried to pinpoint his emotions, and realized he was still angry after all these years. Angry at his mother for one mistake that would last a lifetime. Angry with his father for his constant drinking that, among other things, left Trent and his sister to face this scared, aging world from a young age.

He wondered if Jessica felt like this deep down or if she was really as happy-go-lucky as she appeared. She visited their parents far more than he did, but did seem pretty distraught after the holiday dinner with dad. Understandably so, *but was that an isolated incident, or is she as fucked up as I am?*

Maybe he should talk to her about it, since he was the only one who would understand. But he was kidding himself. He wouldn't talk to her.

A stray breeze pushed against him, and Trenton buried his hands in his pockets, body braced against the cold. The buildings began to grow taller as he made his way closer to the heart of the city. Only a few people walked the streets; most were huddled inside wasting away another Sunday afternoon.

Trenton turned his gaze downward, to the cold, hard ground.

▪▪▪

Another week passed without a word from Molly. Trent went through the perpetual motions of his life, but with Molly avoiding him and his uncertainty surrounding the Resistance, he wasn't sure how long he could hold it together.

He took extra precautions when teaching, and did his best to occupy his mind when he got home. The following weekend, it was finally time to reconvene with the Resistance. He set out around 8:06, hoping that by the end of the night he would finally have some answers.

As he stepped into the station, he became aware of an abnormally large crowd milling about. He searched for a familiar face, and after scanning back and forth several times, spotted the man from the bar. Trent began to walk towards him, but the man looked him in the eye and gave a small shake of his head. In response, Trenton altered his path so that he walked right past the man and out into the street. He headed to a nearby bar hoping to wait out the crowd.

A few drinks later, he felt more relaxed. He had exchanged no more than ten words with any one person, but felt at ease in the noisy bar. When the clock approached eleven, Trenton slid off his stool and made his way back to the PTS station, unsure of what he would find.

The station was now deserted, with the exception of a single man leaning against the left-hand wall. Trent recognized him as the same man that had shook his head at him earlier that evening – the same one from the bar two weeks before who had refused to tell him much more about The Program. The man waved him over and said, "About time you came back. I've been waiting here for hours."

"It was too crowded before. I thought I should wait a while. Won't someone realize something's off if they see you've been down here for so long?"

"Well according to their network, I don't exist. I'm not too worried."

"So you're from outside the city? Can't the cameras see you?"

"Yes, and it's complicated."

"How so?"

"We can hack the system to change footage as it's being stored – you know, overlay a different identity, or even make people disappear. Depends on how likely it is to raise suspicion. As long as we change the footage before The Program analyzes it, we're fine. When a real person looks at it later, they'll be skimming too fast to notice the tampered footage."

"You have all this power? And still haven't gotten anywhere?"

"We've been building up to this for nearly as long as the Program's been in existence. The pieces are just now starting to fall into place."

Trenton considered that for a moment, then asked, "How do you avoid raising suspicion?"

"Well, that's where people like you come in. The internal resistance that we recruited takes care of all that, and they do all the public jobs. Like your pebble drop last fall."

"So we take the risks."

"Yes, because when something big like that happens they're going to find witnesses. If anyone were to see me, and then realize that I'm missing from the records, we would have a much bigger problem on our hands."

Trenton saw the sense in this but couldn't help adding, "You have us do all the dirty work."

"That's the way it has to be for us to remain undiscovered. The only way to destroy The Program is with outside help, at least as far as we can see. Even though we're helping, we're still comically outnumbered and underpowered – because of how difficult it is to get into the City."

"Okay, that all makes sense. But what do you want out of this?"

"The outside world isn't as prosperous as this city. Most rural areas are all but abandoned, with only major cities surviving. Each of these cities has been self-governed ever since the former central government lost control over 20 years ago.

As for why we've decided to help, it boils down to economics. To be frank, our city is on the verge of another depression. Unless something drastic happens, we'll be back in the same place we were twenty years ago. But if we were free to come and go, buying and selling goods and even property, that would be great for our own city. And your government has so much money stored away, a portion of that would be equally helpful. Your government would never allow people to come and go, because it would undermine their Program. The only option is to overthrow the government, which just so happens to help all of you. Not that we aren't looking into other fixes outside your city, but this is our best bet. Now I'd love to tell you more, but you should get moving before anyone notices how long you've been down here."

Trenton was caught off guard by the apparent honesty of the man's response. Based on his knowledge of history, money was a strong motivator, but he doubted it was the only one. Odds were they'd try and screw him over at some point, but he didn't see any other options besides letting things continue on without him. "How do we know you won't come in here and take everything we have once the government is gone?"

"You can't know for sure. But what other choice do you have? At least this way there's a chance of giving your people a better life." And with that, the man pushed him towards the pods, towards the inescapable path that lay in front of him.

CHAPTER FIFTEEN

He gave up. There was nothing worse than the uncertainty, the faint possibility of reconciliation forever hanging over his head. Ready for the worst, he made the call.

Each second seemed unbearably long as he waited for the sound of Molly's voice or, what he really feared, the silence that meant she wouldn't even speak to him. On the last chime, a soft voice answered. "Hi, Trent."

"Molly, I just wanted to apologize for everything. I know you probably don't even want to speak to me..."

"I'm not mad anymore Trent.

"But...?"

"But I'm done."

Those three and a half words (a contraction is basically a word and a half) hit Trent like a sucker punch to the stomach. "I – ok. I'm sorry. I'll let you go."

"Bye."

The call terminated, leaving Trenton to wonder if there was anything he could have done differently. Should he have told her sooner? Waited longer before calling? He ran through each scenario in his mind, analyzed every conversation they'd had, debating if one well-placed word could have made the difference.

He had been sitting at the kitchen table, in the same seat from which she had walked out on him three weeks ago. Now he stood, wrestling with his emotions, while on the outside maintaining the quintessential image of serenity. He managed to keep up the façade for a few minutes, but then the cracks began to appear.

Before he broke down completely, he took a deep breath in an attempt to regain control. He looked out the kitchen window, the uncharacteristically bright winter's day taunting him. "Damn everything," he muttered.

Looking at his ring, he saw the temperature was over 60 degrees. Without further hesitation, he threw on some shorts and an old t-shirt and ran out the door. He took the steps two at a time down to the ground floor, not even slowing as he came out into the lobby, receiving comically dark looks from the few people lounging about.

He ran down the street, head high to catch the breeze on his face, pushing himself to go faster and faster. Within minutes, he was gasping for breath, but he barely slowed his pace as he continued on, relishing the fierce burning sensation that had spread throughout his legs and chest.

He dodged between the few cars that peppered the streets, inciting more than a few angry shouts along the way. His only response was a barking cough that only the most lenient observer would consider a laugh. But seeing as this is not your typical feel-good movie starring a man of slightly below-average intelligence and a wiry physique, Trenton made it only as far as the Screens before pulling up, panting, still far from the city's limits.

Having exhausted all known (and some unknown) reserves of energy, he slowly began the walk back to his apartment. Virtually all feelings had been drained, along with his physical energy, leaving only a single-minded determinedness in their wake. He was ready to act, *compelled* to act. The government wouldn't know what hit them. Ok they would probably know because of their cameras, but they wouldn't be able to stop shit.

When he arrived back at his apartment, he went straight to the shower, enjoying the steady flow of steam and hot water against his back. By the time he had turned off the water, toweled dry, and dressed, the day had aged well into its prime. Trenton itched to go to the bar; after all, it was a Saturday. But he knew he should wait a week. He hadn't exactly been acting normal these last few hours, and he didn't want to draw any attention to himself or the bar.

At that moment, his stomach grumbled loudly, informing him that whatever his plans were, they should be sure to include food. He moved into the kitchen and rummaged through his fridge, looking for anything at all edible. What he found was not overly encouraging: a quarter stick of butter, 3 eggs, a misshapen block of cheddar cheese (it appeared to have been gnawed on, but Trenton didn't remember ever doing such a thing), and some vegetables.

"I guess I'm going out tonight. I'll go shopping tomorrow." He wasn't looking forward to eating out by himself, but he wasn't exactly in the mood for company either. Of course, he hadn't seen Jess in a while, and you could barely consider her company (he meant that in a good way). Before he could change his mind, he made the call.

"Trent! What's up?"

"Just calling to see if you wanted to get dinner. There's nothing in my house to eat and I'm getting hungry."

"Sure! 7:30?"

"Yeah. Where do you want to go?"

"We can just walk the streets and figure it out."

"Jess, it's a Saturday night. We'll get stuck waiting for more than an hour if we don't register ahead."

"Fine, fine. Let's just go to that Italian place down on 2nd."

"Ok, great. I'll notify them," Trent said, already pulling up the restaurant's page through his ring.

"See you in a few!"

The call terminated, and Trent tapped a single button on the holographic screen to notify the restaurant. A screen popped up asking the size of his party and giving him the list of times still available. He quickly filled this out, and the reservation was completed for 7:45, the earliest time he could get.

He considered messaging Jess about the change but quickly thought better of it. This way she might actually be on time.

At 7:28, he pulled on a jacket and made his way to the restaurant. He arrived at 7:40, and was pleasantly surprised to find Jess waiting by the door for him.

"You could have told me the reservation wasn't till 7:45," she said.

"I thought about it, but then I remembered how you're never on time. Plus I did add you to the reservation. If you had checked, it would have given you the exact time"

"You know I never check those things. And hey I was here before you, wasn't I?"

At this moment, their rings dinged, letting them know their table
was ready. As they made their way to their booth with the help of a
waitress, Trenton asked, "But were you here at 7:30?"

Jess took the time to settle into her seat before responding. "No,
7:35." She glared at him as if daring him to comment.

Trent decided he had made his point and let it drop. They
enjoyed a great dinner; Jess toyed with her spaghetti and meatballs while
Trent dug into a savory plate of chicken parmesan. In fact, Trenton was
feeling almost okay until the conversation shifted again.

"You still haven't heard from Molly?" Jessica asked.

Trenton did his best to not react. "I have. It's over."

"Ah shit Trent, that sucks. She seemed pretty great."

Trenton didn't respond, just took another bite of his chicken
parmesan. It really was delicious.

This time it was Jess's turn to change the topic, and soon enough
she was able to bring Trent back to a state of semi-normalcy.

It was nearly 9:30 by the time they left the restaurant and neither
one of them felt much like staying out any longer. They said their
goodbyes, with Jess doing her best to make sure her brother really was
alright (he wasn't, but he'd always been good at hiding it). After a quick
hug, they went their separate ways.

It was only when he'd turned off the lights and slipped into bed
that he remembered the question he'd thought of on his way back from
the prison. He'd wanted to ask her how she really felt about their parents
and, more importantly, if their messed up childhood had left any scars on
her like it had on him. He could still ask her the next time he saw her.
But that wasn't likely.

■■■

As the weeks passed, winter's grip on the city weakened,
sporadically rallying despite it's failing health as it fought for control
against the coming spring. The result was a bewildering weather seesaw;
sunny and 59.0 degrees one day, and 32.2 and dark as night the next.
During the day, not at night. Although it was dark as night *at* night as
well.

Despite the extreme weather fluctuations, Trenton's life
continued on much like it had been, focusing any extra time and energy
on the Resistance. There were no incidents at school and few bad

dreams at night, so Trenton was more or less content. His weekend-morning walks became more frequent and less uncomfortable as the weather slowly improved.

One morning, while out on one such walk, Trenton stopped for a second, enjoying the combination of the nearly hot sun and cool breeze on his face. He looked around at the flawlessly cultivated plants that rimmed the small circular courtyard he had wandered into.

It had been 19 days since he had last spoken with anyone from the Resistance, but it wasn't the long gap in time that occupied his thoughts; he knew the Resistance was very cautious and even with their advanced technology from outside the city, they took as few chances as possible. If and when they needed something from him, they would find him at the bar.

What had kept his mind racing for the past 19 days was what he'd been told at the end of their last meeting: how the Resistance had at least a few people from outside the city, and how their city was slipping into another depression. *What if they take over and nothing changes? They could make their money just as easily that way... I have to hope they're better than that. And they shouldn't need to try that. The excess money our government has stored up, combined with a new rich trade partner, should be enough to kickstart their economy.*

With a start, he realized that he'd been standing motionless for nearly three minutes, and moved on from the courtyard. As he walked, his thoughts rapidly turned back to the Resistance and the possibilities for future end-plans – of which he knew absolutely nothing. As a result, this led to a large amount of thorough and impressively creative speculation. But as imaginative as his ideas may have been, they were ultimately useless.

Giving up his suppositions for the moment, he quickened his pace and made his way back to his apartment. Once he had arrived home, he contemplated his options for the rest of the day and came up empty. There was no girlfriend to see, he had seen Jessica just the other day, and Jason was busy when he called.

"Gotta love being single," he said, resigning himself to another exciting night alone with only The Program or virtual worlds as company. Maybe he needed more friends to keep busy. He gave it a moment's thought and then laughed. No, more friends meant more people. And people sucked.

Better to be bored for a few nights than be forced to go out every night to clubs where you can't even hear yourself speak[1].

Returning to the reality of his shitty evening, Trenton began preparing a light dinner. He took his time, thinly slicing peppers and onions before sautéing them in a pan along with a chicken breast he had plucked from the fridge. As the contents of the pan sizzled away, he grabbed a cold beer and stood over his future meal, alert for any signs of burning.

He switched off the stove when the chicken was suitably browned and sat down to eat, doing his best to ignore the emptiness that pervaded not just the kitchen, but the entire apartment. Once he had finished as much as he could, he turned his attention to the crucial decision of the evening: whether to watch The Program or try his luck at a round of virtual reality.

There was always the "adult" setting on the virtual reality. Quickly, he tapped through the ring's menus, put on the special contact gloves, and lay down on his couch. He spent the rest of his waking hours in the company of a rather too perfect blond, merging fantasy with a twisted version of reality (most of this consisted of just watching and listening – the actual "act" took only 9 minutes and 49 seconds).

Trenton ended the simulation, one part satisfied, one part disgusted, and wholly ready for bed.

---

[1] Those were the only two options obviously. There's no such thing as a middle ground.

"Till death, the fight lasts,
hammering and clawing.
The opponent is living,
is breathing,
is sighing.
"Give up, Give up!"
Winners and Losers shout alike.
As they know.
they know,
to win is still to lose,
and
to lose is fair and
right."
- Random man Trenton passed on the street

CHAPTER SIXTEEN

Trenton was back at The Black Cat, nursing the last few swallows of beer as he waited for a familiar face from the Resistance to approach him. Maybe this would finally be the day he was let in on the plan to take down The Program, and the government along with it.

The last sip of beer was sliding down Trent's throat when the man from the PTS station entered the bar. The man who had told him the Resistance originated outside the city and so much more.

Trenton had never learned his name, which was common when dealing with the Resistance. But the man was so ordinary that Trent had no idea what to call him. Trent caught the man's eye and the man (he really needed to get a name) beckoned with a few fingers from their resting place on the table. Trenton hadn't seen the man since the encounter in the PTS station, more than three weeks ago.

Walking casually over to the man's table, he sat down across from him. "First things first. What can I call you?" Trent asked.

"You can think of me as Savior Jim." The man flashed an amused grin.

Trenton's face remained expressionless. "I'm not calling you that."

Seeing Trent's total lack of reaction, the man relented. "I'm just fucking with you. Call me Jim. But never out loud. Never ever mention me out loud."

"Ok… So am I finally getting clued in about what's going on?"

"Not about everything. Only the first step in our new plan and only in terms of what you need to do. As a heads up, this plan won't be done in a week or even a month. It's going take much longer if we're going to do it right."

"I understand," Trent said, anxious to learn as much as he could.

"Okay. Your first job is pretty simple: we need you to deliver some material to a safe place."

"I'm guessing your not going to tell me what that material is?"

"It's better if you don't know."

"How do I get it? And where am I taking it?"

"You'll find it right here, behind the bar. And as for where you're taking it, you'll learn that next Saturday evening when you're about to move it." With that, Savior Jim stood from the table, not so subtly indicating their conversation was at an end.

Trenton was getting sick of these casual dismissals, not to mention the vague, often unhelpful directions that preceded them. But he bit back a demand for more information, as he was compelled to agree that it was safer for none of the finer details to be known too far in advance.

He stood as well, unable to decide between staying for another drink and heading back to his apartment. He tapped his ring to bring up the home screen, saw the time (10:05), and chose to call it a night. As he walked home, each step seemed to bring him closer to exhaustion; by the time he stood at the foot of his bed, it was all he could do to keep himself from collapsing. With a supreme effort, he walked the four steps to the bathroom. Before closing his eyes for the night, he mechanically fulfilled his pre-sleep routine of teeth brushing, flossing, and relieving himself, in that order.

■ ■

A week had passed with Trenton barely conscious of anything he had said, done, or seen. That probably wasn't a good sign, but hey, he was still here so he must not have fucked up too badly.

He had just walked back into The Black Cat, and was looking for the "material" he was tasked with transporting. The stools on one side of the bar were left vacant and the volume level in the room was just loud enough to mask a quiet conversation. The bartender caught Trent's eye and gestured him to take a seat at the bar. He sat down, hoping the bartender knew more than he did about what came next.

Without encouragement, the man poured him his first drink.

"Where's the thing I'm supposed to be transporting?" Trent asked, finger on his coin, even though by now he was sure the bar must have some sort of protection from The Program.

"It's in here," he said, handing him the glass.

"Wait you want me to *drink* it?" Trent asked, incredulous.

"That's the safest way."

"Hmm. Somehow that sounds like the opposite of safe to me."

The bartender poured himself a glass of water. "All they told me is that it's safer and that we've tested this shit on animals so…

"You've got to be kidding me. Animals?" But Trenton had come too far to let the ingestion of a questionable substance deter him, so he took a gulp of the "material" infused beer, wondering just what the hell he was doing.

"Anyways, it's pretty quiet right now, and everyone in here is vetted. But it'll get busy soon and then we'll have to be careful what we say. You need to be done in less than an hour."

Trenton was too preoccupied with his drink to argue. What was worse was that it tasted strangely good. There was a crispness to it that was more refreshing than a regular beer. Ugh. Something containing strange chemicals shouldn't taste that good.

Trenton did his best to act as if this was just another Saturday night at the bar, but in the back of his mind he was wondering just how many of these he was going to have to drink. And what would the side effects be? But the biggest question was how were they going to remove it from his body? Would they wait for him to pee it out? Would it hurt? Ah fuck.

Squashing his doubts, he finished his first glass without any issues and 6 seconds later, the bartender handed him another. "How many more after this?" Trenton asked quietly when no one else was within earshot (the bar was still mostly empty).

"Four."

Great. Trenton had an okay tolerance, but after six beers he was sure to at least feel something (he wasn't exactly in his prime drinking days anymore[1]). For some reason, he wasn't exactly looking forward to trying to deliver this material – which was now inside his body - to a still unknown location while more than a little drunk.

He downed the second beer in 5 minutes and 10 seconds. Fighting back a grimace, he finished the third and fourth as fast as he could without drawing attention to himself. As the hour grew later, the bar filled up, making it far more difficult to avoid being overheard.

Trent stared at the sixth and final glass, filled to the brim with the special brew. Hoping to steady himself, he took a moment before resuming his drinking. He had a little less than half an hour before his allotted time was up, and he intended to make use of it.

The sixth drink tasted just as good as the first few sips had, but by now his stomach was full and he was starting to feel the effects of the alcohol. After each sip Trent peered into the glass, convinced the glass remained full. In fact, more than the allotted half-hour had passed before he was able to force down the last few drops. The glass now empty, he looked to the bartender, who was now occupied with another customer. When the man finished serving out drinks, Trenton paid him, not knowing what else to do. The man handed him a paper receipt, which was uncommon in this decade, but not overly suspicious.

Trent examined the piece of paper as he exited the bar. Scribbled at the bottom in hastily scrawled script were two words: "Go home." It was hard to be sure, but he guessed that meant… go home. He casually placed the receipt in his pants' pocket and continued down the street, passing one or two people who looked even worse off than him, as well as a few other sober individuals.

By the time Trenton arrived back home, the alcohol had hit him hard. He swayed into the living room, unsure of what to expect. Nothing seemed out of the ordinary, but he wasn't sure if he could trust his dampened senses. After several minutes of stumbling from room to room, Trenton made his way to the bedroom, deciding to give up for the night.

He struggled to undo the buttons on his shirt, his fingers seemingly disconnected from his brain. *Why did I agree to this?* Just as he

---

[1] Let's be honest, he never really drank all that much.

managed to slip into a t-shirt, he heard a door creak somewhere in his apartment. Muted warning sirens went off in his mind. *This is it. What a waste.* Trenton turned to face the bedroom door, saw it slowly sweep open to reveal a man dressed entirely in black.

"Don't say anything. Just get in bed and bring your coin, but don't touch it with your skin." Not seeing the use in disobeying, Trenton did as was asked. The man came the rest of the way into his bedroom. Trenton had never seen this man before in his entire life. Comforting.

The man smirked at Trenton's face. "Relax. I'm here to take your place tonight. We froze the camera in here when you got into bed; we have to be quick so they don't notice anything. Get out of bed now and get dressed. Wear all black. Make sure to hold your coin and then keep it close to you."

"This is so fucking weird," Trenton said. He got out of bed and the stranger got into bed. *His* bed.

"Someone from outside the city is in your living room. They'll take you where you need to go." So Trent walked out into the living room and lo and be hold, there he was, another random-ass man.

The man got straight down to business. "Neither of us can be seen or heard by the cameras right now. I'm communicating with our programmers who are monitoring your path, using The Program, so that we can avoid anyone still out and about."

Trenton was still unsteady on his feet but was pretty sure he could at least follow this man[1] without issue. The two of them made their way out of the building without issue, then began walking. They wound a twisted path through the city, leaving Trenton more and more lost with every turn. Every few minutes they would stop before entering the next street, waiting for a late night passerby... to pass them by. At last, the man pointed to a building up ahead and said "He'll be in there." Then left. Rather abruptly, I might add.

The building was tall and made of steel and glass. So pretty much like every other building in the city. And like most others, there were very few lights shining through the windows at this time of night. Honestly it looked like there was no one there at all[2].

Not knowing what else to do, he walked up to the nearest entrance and knocked softly four times. Shockingly, no one came

---

[1] Who he hoped was *actually* from the Resistance. If he wasn't, then Trent was dead anyways.

[2] Although it would be odd to go through all of this just to send him to an empty building.

running. Trenton hesitated a moment longer, then twisted the handle; the door slid open with ease and Trenton stumbled into the dimly lit lobby.

Trent looked around and saw nothing more than the typical chairs, couches, and the occasional well-placed desk that filled most ground floors in the city. "Hello? Anyone here?" Even though he'd spoken in barely more than a whisper, the surrounding silence amplified his voice twice over.

As the echoes of his questions faded, he waited in the deepening silence for something to happen. He wasn't sure whether he would be excited or terrified when (if) there was some sort of response, but at the moment all he felt was a deep calm and the sudden need to piss.

The seconds stretched out, and just when Trenton was sure there would be no answer, a dark shape appeared on the balcony above him. A thick tenor voice filled the room. "I'm glad you could make it. Please, if you would join me up here, we have much to discuss."

I'm getting really fed up with being ordered around and getting no fucking answers. Trent said out loud, "It would be great to know who the hell you are first, if you don't mind."

The man unleashed a great sigh, as if a child had just asked whether it was all right to run naked in the streets[1].

When Trenton didn't move to ascend the stairs, the man relented, saying, "You deserve to know who I am and what you've been helping with these last few hours. I can explain it all to you upstairs."

Nodding reluctantly, Trent made his way up the stairs. As he stepped onto the second story platform, he got his first good look at the speaker, the light now illuminating his features instead of hiding them. He had dark brown hair and skin even darker. He stood a few inches shorter than Trenton but radiated a natural air of authority. Stepping closer, Trent saw the man held a small metal device loosely in one hand, down by his side.

"Please, sit down," the man said, moving past Trenton, into the room across from the stairs. The double doors leading inside were both open and Trent now saw that the source of light came from within the chamber. The man strode through the doors without another word. Trenton considered staying where he was until he got some answers, but didn't think it would do him much good.

---

[1] Okay maybe that example was a little dramatic, but this is a novel after all. It should have some flair.

He entered the room, took a seat in the proffered chair, and waited. The man sat in his own - noticeably nicer - chair and held up the small instrument Trenton had noticed moments earlier. "Do you know what this is?"

"No, but I'm guessing you're going to tell me. After keeping me in a suspense for a suitable period of time of course."

The man didn't reply, just sat staring at Trenton, metal device in hand. After a lengthy (and uncomfortable) silence, he resumed speaking as if Trenton had never interrupted him. "This is what we like to call a Hacker[1]. It's able to remotely hack into the city's network, showing us what any camera sees in real time. It can also access the location of every single known person in the city by accessing The Program, which uses it's cameras and full body recognition software to do just that."

"And?"

"Take a look." The man handed Trenton the Hacker.

Trent examined the screen, not sure what he was supposed to be looking for. It showed a map of a very small part of the city, with a few black dots marking - Trenton assumed - the locations of citizens in the area. He stared at the small set of interlocking streets and mostly empty buildings. Something clicked into place and he realized the map didn't represent a random part of the city; it represented a very specific section, centered on the exact building in which Trenton sat.

As he focused on the building, he noticed something that seemed to confirm what he'd been told earlier: there were no black dots marking their location in the building.

"How does this work? Does this mean I need to stay out of sight all the time now?"

"No, your invisibility to the Program is tied to your coin – it works with the substance you consumed earlier. You need to touch it and then keep it close to you for this to work."

The man motioned for him to keep it, so Trent stowed it in a pocket. "I still don't understand what I'm supposed to be doing."

The man raised an eyebrow. "Do you really think we'll tell you before we have to?" He was silent for two seconds and then he reached into his back pocket to pull out two dark, metal objects. He handed them to Trenton. "Take these and hide them somewhere safe."

---

[1] Not the most imaginative name, but that seemed to be true of most things in this city…

Feeling their cold weight, Trent realized what they were: a very old-looking gun and silencer. "This thing's ancient. The Resistance doesn't have more modern weapons?"

"This will get the job done. Weapons developed inside the city are all tied to a specific person, as well as the Program. And bringing in weapons from outside the city would raise more questions and cause more problems."

When Trent didn't protest, the man said, "Okay, it's time to go. I doubt you'll see me again. If you need to reach someone, look for Savior Jim[1]."

Trenton allowed himself to be led out of the room, and from there he made his way back to his apartment, alone once more.

[1] Fucking Savior Jim. People really called him that?

CHAPTER SEVENTEEN

Everything had changed for Trenton, yet for the moment, everything was the same. He hid his coin along with the rest of his loot in a pair of worn socks in the back of a dresser drawer and went about his days the same as he always had.

Summer was slowly approaching and with it came the certainty that soon the Resistance would come calling once again. He did his best to distract himself with his work at the Schools and the occasional conversation with Jessica or Jason, but in the back of his mind, he knew he had been given an important role to play. Why else take such a sizeable risk giving him the ability to essentially appear and disappear from The Program at will?

He didn't know if there were others like him, but if he were in charge of the Resistance, he wouldn't want too many people to be able to do such a thing. All it would take is one person abusing it for the government to become suspicious.

This put a sizeable weight on Trenton; there was a significant possibility that when the time came for his part in the Resistance's plan, he would be the only one capable of fulfilling it. There was also a chance he just wanted to feel important and there were ten other guys ready to fill his place. Given the obsessive nature of the Resistance, it wouldn't be that great a revelation.

Now, let's skip past the boring aspects of Trenton's life that you're well accustomed to by now and ahead to next key moment.

Trenton looked over at Savior Jim, who sat next to him at the bar and had assured him that they could speak freely. "You want me to *kill* him? I don't even know where to find him, let alone how to get close to him, *let alone* how to kill him without being seen." Even though he was close to panicking, his voice didn't raise much above a whisper.

"Calm down. You can use the Hacker, and if you pretend to be asleep, we can send someone to lie in your bed, just like last time. Bring the coin with you and be careful not to be seen. It shouldn't be too hard late at night. Then kill him and get back before sunrise."

"Kill him and get back before sunrise," Trenton repeated. "That's very helpful. Shit. How much time do I have to prepare?"

"Three hours. The first two you'll spend at the bar. It happens tonight."

"Of course it fucking does." Trenton slid his hands down his face as he tried to think of any way to murder Brandon Lee, the 2nd in command of The Program Monitoring division, without ending up caught...or so full of bullets, he could be mistaken for a piece of that cheese that has holes in it. You know the kind I'm talking about.

"There shouldn't be any guards, since no one's supposed to know who he is. Guards would just make it clear he's important. Plus the government likes people to think that they're so powerful, they don't need guards.

Trenton didn't say anything in response, just took a very long drink of beer. It was his second and – he had just learned - last beer of the night, so he was going to damn well enjoy it.

Use the stuff you got last time, and wear gloves. After its done leave the weapon with the body."

Jim left the bar, left Trenton to ponder the blood that would be on his hands in approximately 2 hours and 59 minutes.

Trenton managed to nurse the remains of his second beer for the first hour, but then he headed home, watching some boring show on the program to pass the last two hours. They were some of the longest hours of his life (metaphorically speaking. In reality, they were exactly the same length as any other two measured hours).

Finally Trenton carried out his usual nighttime routine, grabbed the sock with the coin in it, and slipped into bed. A door creaked and Trenton was struck by a strong sense of déjà vu. Soft footsteps grew louder until the bedroom door swung open. The man slid into bed next to him (awkward), and Trenton slipped out of bed, coin now in hand. He had smartly left the bathroom light on with the door slightly ajar so that some light bled into the bedroom. Making good use of the dim light, put on black gloves, black pants, and a black long-sleeve shirt with only minimal difficulty. Everyone else was always wearing black, and that was what assassin's wore right? Thinking of what lay ahead, he was glad it was the middle of the night or he would be drenched in sweat the moment he stepped out the door[1].

Now that he was dressed, he rummaged through his open sock drawer for the pistol, silencer, and the Hacker.

He examined the gun, not wanting to get all the way there and not be able to shoot anyone. That would be a damn shame. The gun looked as if it had been designed as much as forty years ago. Trent was not overly familiar with any type of weapon, but he had read about the basics of recent historical firearms. Fumbling around, he managed to check the magazine – full – and find the safety, (which he wisely left on for the moment) without shooting off his foot.

Trenton tried to remember how to use the Hacker. He tapped on the screen[2] and managed to bring up a search bar. He typed in "Brandon Lee" and the screen immediately oriented on a building on the southwest side of the city. It even gave him an exact address.

Returning his attention to the silencer, he practiced screwing it on to the end of the pistol. It took him 1 minute and 17 seconds to get it right. The gun was too bulky as it was to fit in his pocket, and he didn't feel right carrying it out in the open even if it was dark and he was invisible to the cameras. So he unscrewed the silencer and tried reattaching it again, this time managing it in just under a minute. He tried a few more times, getting his time to 21 seconds. That would have to do. He removed the silencer once again and took a deep breath. Then, pocketing the weapon and the Hacker, Trenton thrust himself into motion.

He left his apartment, opening and closing the entrance door as softly as possible, and trusting whoever was fooling the cameras in his room to hide the movement of the door.

When he reached the lobby, he was relieved to find it completely empty. Besides the odd drunk, the streets were similarly deserted. Cautiously, Trenton continued towards his destination, pulling out the Hacker every so often to make sure he was headed in the right direction.

---

[1] Partially from the growing summer heat, but mostly from his nerves.

[2] Yes, a real (presumably) glass screen. That was surprisingly old school for such a powerful device.

He soon arrived in front of the building that contained the black dot of Brandon Lee. Trent fooled around with the Hacker, tapping (in a variety of ways) on the building in an attempt to discover which floor Lee was on. Nothing worked. Without much hope, he tried pinching with his fingers – gratifyingly, the building expanded and turned sideways, showing each individual floor. A thick black line with "Brandon Lee" written over it twitched on the fourth floor. Was he still awake? That would make Trent's job much more difficult. Despite the danger of standing out in the open, Trenton couldn't bring himself to move.

How do I know this guy is even who they say he is? I could be killing an innocent person, or walking right into a trap. But I have to take this chance. I have to end The Program. I can't live with someone watching me for the rest of my life. I can't let everyone forget what it means to be free. If they haven't already. He forced himself to step into the lobby. Thankfully, it was as empty as the rest of the city seemed to be, and Trent had no trouble climbing the four flights of stairs, coming to rest directly outside Lee's apartment door. He attached the silencer to the gun and placed it in the back of his pants with his shirt covering it. From the front, you couldn't even tell.

Feeling as prepared (at least physically) as he ever would, he stood in front of the door, uncertain how to get inside. Somehow, he had glossed over that little detail when preparing for tonight. As he saw it, he had two options. One was to try and shoot the handle off the door, but the sound of a bullet on metal was bound to make more noise than he would like. His other option was to knock, and hope the man was trusting enough[1] to open the door.

He knocked.

A voice came from inside the room. "One minute." The sound of footsteps approached and Trenton could feel the man's eyes on him. "What do you want."

"I just want to talk to you for a minute. My name's Trenton and I work in The Program. Please it will only take a second."

"You don't *look* like you're from The Program."

"Please sir, why would I lie? I'm dressed like this because I'm not supposed to be here, but there's really something you deserve to know."

No further sounds came from inside, but just when Trenton was about to try another tact, the door slowly opened to reveal the stocky figure of Brandon Lee.

---

[1] Or stupid enough.

"Can I come in?" Trenton asked, hoping to avoid making a mess in the hallway.

Lee stepped back, allowing Trent to shuffle inside. The man's apartment was unnaturally tidy. Too bad it wouldn't remain so for long.

Brandon sat down in a big leather recliner. "So what was so important that you had to come dressed like that in the middle of the night?"

Trenton stood a few feet in front of the man, staring into his eyes, asking himself if he was really going to kill this man, who he didn't know at all. Didn't know if he had done even the slightest thing to deserve this death. The only thing he did know was that he'd have to do *something* and he'd have to do it quickly. He couldn't count on the Resistance being able to override the cameras in this man's room, so there was a good chance Lee appeared to be talking to himself. Trenton figured that might raise a few red flags.

Killing this man might help free this city. Was a chance at freedom really worth this (potentially innocent, but more likely guilty) man's life?

Fuck yeah it was.

Trenton reached behind his back with one arm, trying to pull the gun free, but it caught on his shirt. He tugged again and, mercifully, the pistol came free. He brought it around in front of him and said, "You yell or do anything, and you die."

Lee, wide-eyed in shock, nodded fervently. Then Trent squeezed the trigger –
But nothing happened; there was a soft "click" and that was all. Mentally swearing at his stupidity, Trenton flipped the safety.

"You just tried to shoot me!" Lee whimpered, now on the verge of hysterics.

Trenton pulled the trigger again, this time rewarded with a satisfying woosh and thump as the bullet hit just off-center of Lee's chest. He squeezed again, and again, until Brandon Lee's body was littered with holes that each spurted first a fountain, then a stream, and, finally, a steady drip of warm blood.

Looking at the carcass of what had once been Brandon Lee, Trenton tried to feel some kind of remorse, but all he felt was an overwhelming fatigue. He tossed the gun on the floor, checked himself for any bloodstains – there were none – and walked out the door.

He calmly descended to the lobby and strolled out into the night, savoring the slight breeze that blew between the buildings. When he was nearly out of sight, he looked back to see if there was any commotion, but (from the outside at least) everything looked as peaceful as ever.

And Trenton resumed his walk down the street, whistling as he went.

CHAPTER EIGHTEEN

Trenton was startled awake by the sound of sirens for the first time in twenty years. Still groggy from his late-night endeavor the previous evening, he mulled over the meaning of the growing racket. Chances were good they related to him somehow. But all that because of one death? That didn't seem right.

Fighting the urge to drift back to sleep, Trent rose from his bed, grabbing his ring from the bedside table as he went. He threw up a Hologram and flipped to the news, not expecting to find anything remotely informative (or true). Still, with the extra bit of information he was privy to as part of the Resistance, he might be able to piece some of it together.

He walked into the kitchen as a commercial for some energy drink drew to a close and a young female news anchor began to speak. "Hello and welcome back to the city's number one source for all of your news. Today we have a disaster on a scale not seen since before The Program was first established."

I killed one guy, come on, Trenton thought.

The woman continued speaking, oblivious to Trenton's internal dialogue. "Late last night, six government officials were killed by the same number of disturbed individuals working together. I have received word that, using the footage from The Program, the police have already captured all six of the perpetrators and they await their Trials. To protect against the unlikely possibility that there were others working with the criminals, it is advised that no one leave their home alone, and for the foreseeable future, the full force of our security department will be patrolling the streets."

Trenton wasn't sure how to feel. He had assumed that last night had been an isolated incident. No one had actually told him his was the only murder of the night, and it made sense to do as much damage as you could at once, because the government would be on high alert for a long time afterwards. But The Program still appeared to be in place, and the government certainly was, so Trenton wondered how the Resistance would be able to do *anything* now that the government knew of their existence and was rather pissed, to put it mildly.

But that was a question for another day, and for someone else to answer. Today, he should be happy to have been part of such a huge blow against The Program.

He brought his attention back to the news anchor to see if there was anything else worth listening to before he shut off the H-display and set about making breakfast. She was rambling on about various "safety" precautions that would be implemented and Trent was quickly growing bored – the only relevant (and unembellished) piece of information was that the city guards would be actively patrolling the streets at all hours of the day.

Then the anchor shifted focus. "As to the six murderers we have in custody, we've just received word that they are to be tried one each day starting Monday, as a reminder of the cost of betraying The Program, the government, and the people of this city. As always, these will be televised events."

They claimed to have caught all six murderers, and yet here Trenton was, straight chillin' in his apartment. So were all six "criminals" just normal people being used as scapegoats? If so, Trent was in for a long week.

Having heard enough, he turned off the holographic screen and began preparing his usual morning meal of three sunny-side-up eggs and bacon.

■■■

Trenton's ring dinged again and a small hologram popped up with the face of the caller: it was Jess. Unfortunately, Trenton was not currently wearing his ring. Or even in the same room, as he was far too busy clogging up his only toilet. Six minutes later, Trenton finally exited the bathroom, leaving the toilet to its cruel fate. Jessica chose that moment to call again and this time Trenton looked over as his ring erupted in another frenzy of activity.

He strode over, and slipped on his ring. "Jess. What's up?"

"Hey, so kind of you to pick up after ignoring my last two calls."

"I was in the bathroom…"

"Uhuh. Taking an oversized dump I bet. Have you been watching the news?" Her voice was softer than usual. Almost subdued, though the all too accurate reference to his bowel movement was a reassuringly Jess-like comment.

"I heard about the murders and government's response if that's what you mean."

"Its crazy, what's happening. They've already tried two of them. It's sickening."

"Yeah." Trenton had watched the first trial but the knowledge that he was partially responsible for the mutilation of these innocent people left him in a decidedly sorry state. Watching innocent people pay for his actions affected him in a way that murdering someone connected to The Program hadn't. He had thought better of watching the second trial that had been televised earlier today.

"You around tonight?"

"Yeah, you want to get dinner?"

"Let's just hangout and eat food at my place. I need some company. You gonna be okay getting over here alone?"

"Jess, I'm sure I'll be fine. I'll head over now." He hung up, threw on some shoes and practically flew out the door.

The streets *were* different now. On every corner, policemen surveyed the passing cars and pedestrians, alert for anything out of the ordinary. Although the streets had always been monitored with cameras, the physical presence of the guards created an entirely new atmosphere on the street. In some ways, Trenton actually preferred it this way; at least now it was harder to fool yourself that no one was watching.

Trenton kept his head down and walked speedily to the nearest PTS station. Six minutes later, he had arrived at Jess's building and was inside her apartment a minute after that.

Jess hugged him as he came through the door and then they both took a seat on the couch. Trent thought about what could serve as a good distraction. The Program was probably not a good idea. "How about a movie night?"

Jess brightened a little at the suggestion. "Oh yeah. That sounds perfect. And we can order greasy pizza!"

"Mmmmm. Grease," Trent said. "My favorite food." He had begun searching for a movie with his ring, going through the extensive back catalogue the city had stored. People spent so much time watching The Program, which needed no writers or directors and made copious amounts of money, leaving little reason to fund any new films. By Trent's reckoning, the last good movie had been released eighteen years ago.

While Trenton was methodically searching for a movie, Jess proceeded to order a pepperoni and meatball pizza (grease included) to be delivered to her apartment. Once she had taken care of the food, Jess joined Trent in the search for the ideal movie.

Twenty-one minutes later, the pizza had arrived, and they still couldn't agree. "Fine, just pick something that isn't *too* boring," Trent relented.

Jess eventually decided on a romantic-comedy (of course) and they spent the next two hours and five minutes engrossed in the spectacle before them, doing their best to forget the police that patrolled the streets, forget the torture of innocent men who were suffering for the Resistance's actions.

Most of all, they tried to forget the cameras that watched, judged, and revealed everything to all.

When the credits started to roll, neither of the two siblings moved to turn off the screen. They sat together, silent until the last name had disappeared, leaving behind only darkness.

Trenton was about to excuse himself for the night when Jess began to speak. "Do you ever wonder what our lives might've been like if dad hadn't been a drunk? I think about that way too much."

Caught off guard, Trent struggled to string a sentence together. And failed miserably.

Luckily, Jess resumed speaking without any help from Trenton, determined to – at long last – discuss their less-than-ideal childhood. "I barely remember anything about the world before The Program. I was only six when it went into effect. It was right around then that dad started drinking, so I hardly remember the old him either.

"Most of what I remember came afterwards, when everything went to shit. Shouting matches, missed soccer games, whispered rumors at school about what mom had done and how dad drank more alcohol than water. Those are the things I remember most. And once The Program did a piece on our family because it was just too tempting to ignore, things got even worse. But you know all about that."

"How do you feel about mom and dad now? You spend much more time with them than I do," Trent said, finding his tongue.

"I still resent them for what they put us through, but I'm trying to forgive them. Dad doesn't make it easy, but mom really does regret what she did to us. I know I hide it really well, but I'm still pretty fucked up. I'm sure it's a large part of the reason why all my good relationships fall to pieces."

Trent searched Jess's face in the almost non-existent light, but her head was still turned towards the H-Display and he wasn't able to see much of anything. Trying to provoke a smile he said, "Hey I'm pretty fucked up too. You can't hog *all* the attention just cause you're the younger sister."

"Very funny Trent. But you seem to be doing just fine from what I can see."

"You seemed to be doing fine too. Clearly we're too good at hiding our shit for our own good."

Jess's response was to turn towards him and pull him into a violent hug. "Thanks, Trent," she said, her voice muffled by the fabric of his shirt.

"I'm just sorry I didn't bring it up before. From now on I'll try to talk more about how I'm actually feeling. Not promising I'll share everything but I'll make more of an effort. Baby steps."

He could hear her smirk as she replied. "Yeah, wouldn't want to bring either of us *too* far out of our comfort zones."

"Of course not," Trent said. "Alright, I should get going, but if you need to talk, message me. And I'll do the same."

"Sounds good."

Trent left Jess's apartment, feeling better than he had in three weeks.

CHAPTER NINETEEN

It was Wednesday, more than four days since the murders, but as Trenton glumly surveyed the classroom, he couldn't fail to notice the array of empty seats. He had expected some parents to hold on to their kids on Monday, but this was growing out of control. On one hand, he understood. What had happened had been "horrible", and the aftereffects were still being felt, what with the police everywhere and the ongoing trials. But as a teacher, he had a job to do. And when a quarter of the kids failed to show up three days in a row (with even more students missing those first two days), that made his job that much harder. The government should have cancelled school, but they probably didn't want to cause even more worry – there hadn't been an unscheduled cancellation in years.

"All of you that decided to show up today, thank you. I know how difficult this week has been. I'm expected to teach a certain set of material before the end of the year, and we can't afford to waste any more time. I hate to do this, but please let your classmates know that everything we cover in class today will be required as homework for tomorrow. It may be sent in electronically if they continue to be effected by last weekend's tragedy. I have to continue to teach this class despite what is happening outside the classroom."

One or two students let out a groan, but for the most part they remained silent, knowing he had a point. He began lecturing, pretending that he wasn't teaching to an artificially diminished class and that he wasn't partially responsible.

He was true to his word, and after finishing the lecture, he navigated his way through the menus on the board to extract a copy of today's footage. When he was sure the video contained everything of import from the lesson, he said, "Send this to all missing students. If they don't watch it in it's entirety, and write up their own notes, they will fail for today." His ring, the real source of most of the processing power behind the board, dinged in acknowledgement and a message popped up, confirming his demand.

The missing students would understand this was no idle threat, as The Program would now inform him of anyone who ignored his assignment. While he didn't have personal access to any of the footage, someone or something (he wasn't really sure which) would now be actively monitoring the kids for the next 24 hours.

This led him to another tangential thought. Much like crimes, cheating was now a thing of the past because of the 99.99% certainty of getting caught[1]. In those first few years while Trenton was still a student himself, he'd heard of many students trying their luck, believing The Program wasn't as powerful as the government led them to believe. Sometimes it took up to a week, but eventually every single one of them got caught (well he wouldn't have known if anyone got away with it but from way everyone acted (and the grades everyone got) he seriously doubted it).

But what was your integrity and character worth when the only reason you acted properly was out of fear?

Trenton brought his attention back to the now empty classroom, wondered what he was still doing here, and left the room without a backwards glance.

Ever the thoughtful totalitarian authority, the government had scheduled each trial to take place at different times of the day, so that *everyone* would get a chance to see at least one. Monday's had been in the morning at 8:00 am, Tuesday's at 12:00, so you could enjoy it on your lunch break, and Wednesday's (today), was at 3:30, giving students enough time to get home from school and enjoy the show.

In an attempt to miss today's trial, Trenton stayed behind after his last class, doing some work from school that he could have just as easily done from home. When he deemed that enough time had passed to avoid viewing the trial, he shut off the H-display and keyboard he had been using, and started back to his apartment.

Trenton arrived home and flipped on an H-display, 96% confident the Trial was over for today.

---

* Not a real statistic whatsoever – but Trenton thought it was a good guess

The screen showed the bloody remains of a body, restrained in a metal chair. The only sign of life was the movement of the chest barely noticeable, marking the passage of air in and out of the lungs. Based on the feminine shape of the body and the wispy shoulder length hair, Trenton assumed he was looking at a woman, but it wasn't entirely clear. Fresh blood covered most of what was left of the body, which had numerous pieces missing from it.

For a moment, Trenton saw his sister, then Molly, sitting slumped in the chair. He forced that image away, *knowing* it had to be false. He forced himself to look closer at the body – and was sure he didn't recognize it.

He released a long breath as the woman was unstrapped from the chair and led out of the room to wherever the government put all their Trial-worthy criminals. They never killed them on-screen[1] and claimed they were locked up for the rest of their lives. All Trent knew was that after your trial, you had approximately zero chance of ever being seen again.

Trent checked the time: it was nearly 4:30. That must have been an abnormally long Trial - usually they went on for less than half an hour. Suppressing a shudder, Trenton imagined the prolonged agony that the government's latest victim must have endured.

The screen switched back to the regular programming now that the Trial was over. It was a comedy show, the only one worth watching. Not exactly the kind of show he wanted to watch after what he had just witnessed, but he left it on anyway. Maybe it could help him forget about all this shit for a little while.

Not for the first time that day, he found himself wishing Molly were sitting next to him. He tapped his ring to bring up her profile. His finger hovered in front of the call button for a solid six seconds. Then he slowly dropped his hand, returning his attention to The Program.

---

[1] Well it happened very rarely and only if they waited too long to give them medical attention or slipped up with one of the power tools – you know, honest mistakes.

CHAPTER TWENTY

Trenton sat at the bar, both hands wrapped around his drink. Dark shadows painted the undersides of his eyes. Only three days had passed since he'd witnessed the last few moments of the Trial with the female "rebel and murderer." Wait, shouldn't it be murderess? He checked his ring. It *was* murderess. *And here I am thinking the government must be pretty smart to have kept control the last 20 years. But nope, they can't even use the right word to describe the people they're torturing. That's just sad.*

He gulped down another sip of beer and chuckled grimly. After the trial of the *murderess* on Wednesday, he had forced himself to watch the last three trials. He had to know if anyone he knew was being tortured. Not to mention the innocent people being punished deserved at least that much from the one (partially) responsible for their "situation". Needless to say, he hadn't handled it very well. He had considered staying home tonight, but he needed to know for sure whether the people the government had tortured were involved with the Resistance at all.

At long last, Savior Jim walked through the door and took a seat at his customary table. Seeing Trent, he shook his head slightly, and looked towards the door. Trent debated flinging his mug at the man in frustration, but restrained himself. Didn't want to waste those last few sips of beer still in the glass.

Swallowing his anger (and the rest of his beer), Trenton stood and lumbered out of the bar. The humid night air warned of the quickly approaching summer, but Trenton was in no mood for warnings.

A substantial number of people still roamed the streets – it was 9:35pm. No one paid him any attention. They were too wrapped up in their own lives to waste their time on a half-drunk stranger passing by in the street. Even the police hardly spared him a glance, and that was just fine by Trenton. He sure as hell didn't want any extra attention.

He let his feet wander, too anxious to head home, but unsure of where else to go. But he was far less relaxed with his mind, forcing it to focus on thoughts about the Resistance, the trials, and his role in *everything*. Honestly, there was so much metaphorical shit to wade through it was astounding he could think at all.

After about 27 minutes of this, Trenton stopped mid-step. The crowd around him had thinned considerably with only a few stray people left hurrying on their way. One or two looked over curiously when Trent stopped, one foot hanging in the air, but they soon returned to their own concerns. Inch by inch, he lowered his foot to the ground. Then he pivoted on his heels and continued on in the opposite direction, footsteps thudding steadily onto the concrete below him.

He retraced his steps, a hint of an idea tickling his pre-frontal cortex[1]. What if all this was for nothing? What if people really were better off the way things were now? No, he had come too far, gotten too close to give up now. The government may have brainwashed the majority of the population into accepting The Program, but that didn't mean they were truly happy the way things were.

He had reached a turning point. Literally. The road in front of him broke into a four-way intersection. One of those paths led nowhere of interest, and he had just come from another. That left two choices, straight, or to the right. Straight led in the direction of the bar as well as his apartment, while the right path led to the unknown (in that Trenton rarely found himself in that section of the city). Trent didn't think he should go back to the bar, and he wasn't quite ready for bed, so without further deliberation, he took a stroll down the right-hand path[2].

Most of the buildings in this area were dark (they were office buildings so that made sense at this time of night) and though the streets were well lit, the silent, towering shadows created an eerie atmosphere.

There were no guards on this particular street, which wasn't too surprising. The city may have been on high alert, but there weren't enough guards to keep constant watch on every street. He shared the road with a single old man, who seemed lost in his own head.

[1] Or maybe it was his hypothalamus, he really had no clue.

[2] For any of you thinking the intersection is a metaphor, don't go all analytical on me.

Trenton touched the coin in his pocket, rendering himself invisible to the cameras. Carefully looking both ways, Trenton walked out into the middle of the road. He stood there for about a minute and when no cars materialized, he promptly lay down on his back. In the middle of the road. *Wonder what would happen if I fell asleep right now.* He giggled at the thought.

He rolled his head around on the ground, taking in his surroundings. The old man looked over at Trent, shook his head, and continued on his way.

For a brief second, Trenton wondered just what the hell he, Alex Eustacias Trenton, was doing. Then he shouted at the old man from the comfort of his cement bed. "Hey! I'm trying to sleep here! Can't a man take a nap without being disturbed?"

Instead of responding, the man hurried his step and avoided looking anywhere near the road in which Trenton lay.

When the man was no longer in sight, Trenton closed his eyes and rolled onto his stomach. A second later, he shivered, jolting himself out of... whatever that was, and jumped to his feet. "Shit. Shit shit shit *shit.*" A light misting rain began to fall. Because why not.

I'm way more fucked up then I thought. I'm fucked up in every way I can think of. What was I doing?? No one besides that old man had seen this little show (that he knew of), so there was a chance he wasn't totally screwed. But he was probably screwed. For now, he just wanted to find his way back to the familiarity and dryness of his apartment. Fortunately, the air was still warm even with the delicate rain drizzling down so Trenton wasn't cold *and* wet. Just wet. He soon reached the intersection that had so enthralled him on his walk earlier in the night.

The choice was simple now. In fact, some might say it had become no choice at all. Without pause, he turned down the right fork towards his apartment[1].

■■

It was Sunday. 12:05 pm. Trenton had been awake for a few hours and was playing a round of holographic mini-golf in his living room when he heard a clunk and a click behind him. He turned around

---

[1] The bar lay in that direction as well, but was undoubtedly closed by now and Trenton had had enough to drink for one night.

to see his apartment door swing open. Without thinking, Trent brandished the golf club in his hands – as Savior Jim stepped inside. Jim arched an eyebrow at the raised club and Trenton remembered it was a simple hologram that only felt solid in his hands because of the gloves he wore. He lowered the club.

Savior closed the door firmly behind him. "So you wanted to talk to me at the bar last night. There were some people we weren't sure about hanging around so I figured I'd stop by today to talk to you. We've taken care of the cameras in here for the next hour."

"Wow, a personal visit. You don't know how lucky I feel," Trenton said, the sarcasm thick in his voice. "How exactly are you getting around in daylight?"

"I'm not a vampire, Trent. But if you're referring to the fact that I'm invisible to cameras and someone on the street may report a man who isn't anywhere in The Program, there's little chance of that happening unless some big event goes on. The security may be tighter, but I don't exactly stand out in a crowd."

Trenton couldn't help but agree, remembering how hard it had been to assign the man a nickname, what with his absence of distinctive features. He was decidedly average in every (physical) way.

"I need to know if the people the government Tried last week were all innocents. I'm guessing they are, but not knowing for sure is getting to me. You don't even want to know what I did last night. Unless you know already."

"We saw, and luckily it seems we were the only ones. Aside from that old man and so far he's said nothing." Jim looked down at the floor, his mouth pressed into a thin line. "As for the people put on trial last week, it doesn't appear that any of them were involved in the Resistance or committed any crime whatsoever."

"So they died because of us. Because of what we did."

"No. They died because of the government. It was the government trying to punish us, trying to force our hand. If our plan succeeds, no one will ever have to face a Trial like that again."

Trent's fingers twitched inside their gloves. "Oh yeah. The plan. I'm getting tired of doing all this shit with no explanation, with all of you claiming 'it's part of the plan.'"

"Trust me Trenton, this is hard for me too." Jim paused for a second, then said, "Listen, because of what we did – getting rid of those government officials – The Program has never been weaker. Those men were in charge of key parts of The Program. Sure, they'll be replaced, but they were put in place for a reason. With them gone, the Government will be put off-balance. And by off-balance, just picture a huge, immovable mountain that is now slightly smaller, but still pretty damn massive. It all depends on how the rest of the plan plays out. If we're smart and really lucky, we might be able to make sure that when the time comes to end this, it'll stay – uh – ended.

"I'm here to give you more information about the next step, if you want to be a part of it. The only way those peoples' Trials and the deaths we caused will mean anything, is if we finish this. So will you see this through?"

"Like I even have a choice at this point?"

"There's always a choice. We need to know we can count on you."

Trenton considered for half a second. He thought back to the Trials and the horrible stress it caused him, triggering the downward spiral that had taken place. That had ended with him sprawled in the middle of the road, which was an unsettling outcome to say the least. Somehow he doubted that was the worst he would do or have done to him[1]. "I'm in."

"Good, because we could use all the help we can get. We'll need to get the support of the people if we're going to have any chance of overthrowing the government. We need to find some way to let everyone know in greater detail what the government has been up to. How they torture innocent people. We must remind everyone how the government profits off of our "private" lives, recording us as we sleep, use the bathroom, have sex. Then they sell it to the highest bidding cable networks. We have to explain that things weren't always this way and they don't *have* to be this way.

"We don't want to give away the ace in our hand – our growing control of The Program – so we need to find a more low-tech way of getting the truth out. We already have some ideas but we want your input. The overarching plan is in place, but this intermediary step has to be damn-near perfect if we're going to have a real chance at getting the people on our side."

Trent nodded his head.

---

[1] Anyone wondering how he packed so many words into half a second of thinking should try timing their thoughts (good luck with that). They can be damn quick.

"Think on it for a few days. 12:00 AM on Wednesday night a few people from outside the city will come by your house and we'll make our decision," Savior Jim said. He reached behind him for the doorknob, grappled with it briefly, then swung it open and swept out of the room.

CHAPTER TWENTY-ONE

The next few days passed by on autopilot as Trenton spent all of his remaining brainpower on the problem at hand: how to get the Resistance's message to as many people as possible and as effectively as possible *without* giving away their increasing power over The Program. Maybe he should bake a cake too.

In order to increase his chance of success, he invented as many scenarios as he could and agonized over the ramifications of each one. The first few that came to mind were relatively simple, but as he approached the last of the three days before the meeting, they grew more and more complex. About four hours before the meeting was set to start, Trent went over the most viable plans he had come up with.

His ideas ranged from writing messages on sidewalks and walls, to commandeering the entire plaza containing the Screens. To be honest, most of his ideas were crap. Soon enough the four other members trickled in, minutes apart so as to more easily avoid attention[1].

Trenton waited for that last minute burst of inspiration that occurs in every pop novel. None came (remember this isn't a shitty pop novel, it's much, much more). By now everyone had taken a seat in the living room. From his perch on the edge of the couch, he examined the faces of his fellow resistance members.

They were an interesting bunch. The man on Trenton's left had a thick black mustache with specks of gray and white. He looked to be the oldest by a few years. The woman who had been last to arrive sat across from Trent, her wavy blond hair and pale skin the brightest things in the room, aside from the lights themselves.

---

[1] That wasn't the only security measure, but it was the only one he noticed.

The other two were nearly as average in appearance as Savior Jim, one dark-skinned, one light. Trent didn't even attempt to examine them beyond this shallow observation, knowing how futile it would be.

Trenton was about to speak when Moustache Man beat him to it. "We all know why we're here. We'll each present the best idea we've thought of, and then, after everyone has had a chance to ask questions about each of the other plans we'll vote on the best one."

The dark-skinned ordinary-looking man piped up at this point, laying out his proposal. "I believe we should modify more PTS stations like the one that blocks signals to the rings and feeds false video to the cameras. Then we could put posters and messages up in these stations so that many people would see them on their commute before any government official noticed and took them down."

The group considered his suggestion silently for a healthy minute. Trenton was the first to respond. "But if we modify that many PTS stations, won't the government realize that we're hacking into The Program? I'm not a tech guy – I don't know how that all works, but wouldn't that be a problem?"

The girl across from Trent scowled in his direction with remarkable vehemence. "It wouldn't necessarily have to be a wide-scale hack." She bit off each word as if it were hardened taffy. "We could use a different approach that could be done locally at each station; it wouldn't be too difficult and wouldn't reveal too much either."

"But will people really pay attention to some random posters on their way to work?" The white, ordinary-looking man spoke for the first time. "And will it have any real impact on how they view The Program?"

Moustache Man spoke up again. "It could if we get their attention somehow and remind them of the truths they've forgotten, or prettied up. The reality of The Program and what the government is doing will be enough to at least plant some doubt in many of their heads."

The first idea concerning the PTS stations finally broke through some barrier in Trenton's clogged skull and an idea rose to the surface, fully formed as if it had been percolating all this time, just waiting for the right moment to reveal itself.

When no other responses were forthcoming, Trent began explaining his own insidiously genius plan. Whatever the hell that means. "My idea is deceptively simple. We find out as much as we can about the six victims of the Trials, and just post it everywhere. We make their names – and their deaths - mean something. We get their friends and family to talk to us – we let the world know that they were never involved in the Resistance, and were no worse than you or your neighbor, your sister or brother. We do that, and we won't even have to mention anything else the government is doing wrong. That would just take attention away from the torturing and – for all intents and purposes – deaths, of six innocent members of this city."

"So you want to make them into martyrs." Tapping a finger on his thigh, Moustache man thought through Trenton's idea. "It's a good plan but the government is always very careful to not release the names or anything else about anyone on Trial for this very reason."

Trenton had already thought of this. "We could get that information from The Program pretty easily right? The government would have no idea how we got it – from their perspective, it could be possible that we had asked around and found out how to contact their friends and family, or that we personally knew some of the victims. Compared to actually overriding part of The Program, this seems a lot less risky."

The Moustache Man nodded. "And they already know they can't trust their surveillance to catch us because of the deaths we caused. They wouldn't be learning anything new about us at all from this."

"But where do we actually put up the information?" Ordinary White Guy asked. "Out on the streets? Or down in the PTS stations like the other plan suggested?"

"I think it depends on how many people we can get to help. We could take the cameras down in the stations for a few hours, but we'd only have one night to get everything set up. So unless we have a lot of people working with us, there's no way we'd be able to cover enough of the city before the police tear everything down in the morning," Moustache Man said. He looked to the blond-haired woman as if she had more information.

She caught the hint and said, "Our size is kept purposefully vague. I know there's more than ten of us and less than fifty, but that's all."

"So if we assume at most twenty people will be able to help on the actual night, would we be able to cover most of the city in three hours?" Moustache Man asked.

The woman shook her head and the Ordinary Black Guy said, "I'm not sure we could even do it with fifty."

"And we're forgetting about the guards that still patrol the streets. That will make things even more difficult," Moustache Man added.

Trenton broke in again. "That's why we should use the PTS stations like the first guy said. That way we can avoid the guards, feasibly covering all the stations, and pretty much everyone funnels through them in the morning."

The conversation continued on, ironing out the fine details for a number of hours, but by the end of the night they had agreed on a course of action. In a week and one day (that would be the following Thursday for those of you not following along), they would act.

■■

It was still Wednesday, though a different Wednesday than in the above paragraph. This was the Wednesday before the instigation of the plan. Trenton's stomach had become increasingly unsettled these last few hours. He had done his best to ignore it, but he could do so no longer. Giving in, he burped a sour-tasting (and smelling) burp - and felt only a little better. He tried piecing together what was really bothering him and discovered he was *nervous*. Well shit.

There must be something wrong with me, Trenton thought. *I'm more nervous about this then I was about killing a guy.*

Still, back then the government had been more lax, trusting The Program to protect them from most threats. Now police patrolled the streets, watching. Even at night there were guards, though much fewer than during the day. Not to mention he'd had a week to think about what could go wrong.

Trenton snapped back to reality[1] and looked down at the small plant by his feet. He was standing in one of the city's gardens after finishing up at school. The garden was sparsely populated with people as most were either still at work or congregating in the more urban areas of the city.

Of all the plants that filled the garden, the only one Trent saw was the fragile fern directly in front of him. He was drawn to it. At first, it appeared to be indistinguishable from the other ferns. But when he

[1] Yes, that was a reference to a fantastic rap song.

looked closer, the true state of things became evident. Underneath the outer layer of green leaves, were spots of brown. And as you moved to the lowest inner level of the plant, only death and decay remained.

CHAPTER TWENTY-TWO

Black outlines flitted through the streets, avoiding guards and streetlights. Luckily, these shadows didn't have far to go. Each one came from a different direction and carefully traveled to the PTS station closest to them.

When Trenton reached his station a shadow already stood waiting inside. His body tense, he cautiously stepped out into the light of the inner station – and saw the blond-haired woman from the meeting. Trenton relaxed a fraction. "For a second, I thought you were a guard," he whispered.

She gave him a condescending look. "I've already set up the camera blocker. It's in my pocket – we'll secure it here when we finish for the night," she said as she moved to open the emergency access panel in the far corner of the room. She twisted the circular access mechanism and, together with Trenton, lifted the hatch to reveal a black hole of space.

The woman pulled out the miniature (and archaic) flashlight that had been distributed to each pair of resistance members. Each of them was carrying a heavy backpack filled with pictures of the six victims from the trials, along with stories from their lives.

"Shouldn't we do this one first?" Trent asked, looking around the station.

"No. We'll do it last." Before Trenton could ask for an explanation, she had disappeared down the hole. "Close the hatch when you come down." Her voice echoed up to him. "If someone walks in here, that would be a dead giveaway that's something's going on."

"Oh, I was planning on leaving it open for anyone to walk in and see." But she was already gone, leaving no other option than to follow her down the aluminum ladder. With each passing rung, his body plunged further into the cool blackness of the subterranean hole. He dutifully closed the hatch as his head dropped below ground level, and was left in near total darkness. The only surviving light was the narrow beam of the woman's flashlight, uncomfortably far below.

Trent concentrated on the simple motion of descending the ladder. He grabbed tightly to each rung as he went, comforted by the sharp bite of metal cutting into his sweaty palms.

After an indeterminable amount of time stuck in this rhythm, Trenton brought his foot down – and found solid concrete. He tapped around with his foot, ensuring he was in fact at the bottom, and was satisfied with the thick smacks that resulted. Relaxing his shoulders, he lowered his other foot to the ground and looked around for his partner.

She was standing a few feet away, shaking her head impatiently as she watched him get his bearings. "Ready?" she asked.

"Yeah." There were tunnels branching out in all directions. Trenton knew there were many paths to each nearby PTS station so that individual pods could avoid creating traffic. It was a brilliant system – except for when you were trying to find your way by foot. Thankfully, Trenton hadn't been tasked with navigation. Blondy carried the map, along with the flashlight[1], and having picked out the right tunnel, she began moving through it. Trent was left once again to follow along.

"You know, I get the feeling you're not too impressed with me," Trent whispered as he jogged to catch up.

"Hmm. You must have good instincts to figure that out all on your own," her voice dripped with sarcasm, but Trenton swore he saw her crack part of a smile. *Probably just a trick of the light,* he thought. *There's no way that girl is capable of smiling.*

Soon they reached another ladder and climbed up to enshrine their first PTS station. For the first time Trenton was ahead, and as he reached the top, his partner tugged on his arm, gesturing for him to wait. She dove into a separate compartment of her backpack and pulled out a palm-sized disc. Holding down a single button to turn it on, she handed it up to Trent, who used copious amounts of Duct Tape[2] to attach it to the underside of the trapdoor.

---

[1] On the other hand, he wouldn't have minded being in control of the flashlight. Whenever he fell behind, the darkness was stifling.

[2] Yes, Duct Tape is still a thing in the future. How could it not be?

"That's pretty low-tech so it'll only play back previously recorded footage – it won't fool anyone for long, but it only needs to give us till tomorrow morning," Blondy said, uncharacteristically helpful.

Trent grunted his understanding and carefully twisted open the hatch. He peered around the room, alert for anything unusual[1]. Seeing no one, he clambered out and offered a hand to Blondy, which she blatantly ignored.

They left the hatch open and threw open their backpacks, grabbing one of the folders the Resistance had put together. Each folder had one copy of all the material they had decided on. They worked in tandem, pasting pictures, and large headlines. Neither one kept watch, instead moving as fast as possible to finish the job. In all, it took them 8 minutes and 16 seconds to set everything up.

Trenton was securing the last poster when Blondy soundlessly slipped back down the emergency hatch. He sighed and scrambled after her.

Back in the underground tunnel system, Trenton grunted. "Is this how the next three hours are going to go? You running around, not talking to me, and basically just pissing me off?"

"Yeah that sounds about right," Blondy replied without turning around.

"I don't know what's up your ass, but could we actually work together and get this done without either of us dying and/or blowing the mission?" Trent caught up to her and matched her pace, and – to his shock – she actually looked over at him.

"I think I can do that, but you have to keep up." She looked down at the map to ensure they were still on track and then said, "Oh, and there's nothing up my ass by the way. I try to avoid that."

Trenton had no idea if that was supposed to be a joke, so he stayed silent just to be safe. A moment later the beam of the flashlight reflected off the second ladder, and they commenced another ascent. They set up this second station identical to the first (give or take a few inches) and cut 28 seconds off their time.

About 45 minutes had passed and they still had another five stations to do, including the one they had left for last. That put them on track to finish before the three-hour deadline, but Blondy didn't let up.

---

[1] By unusual, I assume he meant a guard looking to kill or seriously injure them.

They finished another two stations in 40 minutes without any issues. Blondy even complemented Trenton on his newfound speed. She may have been saying it sarcastically, but Trent took it as a win.

Unfortunately, Trent started to tire soon after this, his endurance not as impressive as it had once been. The blond-haired woman started to pull ahead again. They reached the next ladder with her in the lead and she scurried to reach the top before Trenton had climbed even halfway. Blondy attached a disk to the underside of the hatch, opened it a crack, and looked around. Seeing the way was clear, she jumped out and began posting the usual material. 59 seconds later, Trenton joined her.

They tore through their respective folders, hastily putting up the same pictures and poignant stories that would soon be in nearly every PTS station in the city. When they were finished, Blondy once again beat him down the hole. Trent imagined himself in bed asleep, but quickly shook himself out of that preposterous fantasy and followed his partner back down the ladder.

There were only two more stations left to cover and about an hour to do so. Trent was still lagging slightly behind, but pushed himself in order to stay within the radiating light of the flashlight. The journey through the tunnels felt noticeably longer than the others, but it may have been a byproduct of Trenton's growing exhaustion.

The ladder ultimately came into sight, Blondy no more than a shadow carrying a light as she made her way up to ground level. Trenton gathered his energy at the base, then started up after her.

The hatch was open when he reached the top, but the murmur of voices kept Trent from barreling out into the open. He inched his head up above the level of the hole, and grimaced at the scene playing out before him. Blondy stood, hands raised, with a guard pointing a standard issue pistol[1] directly at her chest. The officer was growing increasingly agitated. He said, "I want to know what the fuck you were doing down there, and I want to know it now. If you don't answer, I'm going to call the whole force down here."

Blondy was slowly walking in a circle away from the emergency hatch and the guard turned to keep her in line with his weapon. In a moment, the guard's back was to the hole, and more importantly, to Trenton.

---

[1] Each pistol was paired with a guard so that no one else could make use of it. The simple act of unholstering it notified the Program, and firing it notified every guard within a mile radius. Hopefully the Resistance was able to fully block that signal…

Trenton carefully extricated himself from the hole, and edged towards the officer. The man twitched as if he had heard something - and before he could think better of it, Trenton dove on the guard from behind, knocking them both the ground. He reached for the man's head to slam it on the tiled floor, but before he could do anything, an elbow flashed towards his face, and the world spun as he fell backwards.

Trent wrestled with his own body, trying to get to his feet. His vision cleared to reveal Blondy standing over the unmoving body of the guard. The man was either unconscious or dead, and Blondy was visibly trembling with either shock or fear or disgust. Or perhaps some combination of the three. The gun lay unnoticed and unneeded, five feet away.

Shuffling over, Trenton did his best approximation of checking for a pulse. To his surprise he managed to find it. "He's still alive." He looked up at his partner. "What do we do?"

She shook her head. Trenton thought it through out loud. "He might be able to identify us if we leave him. Or at least me, since I'm still part of The Program. So we either bring him with us, or we kill him."

Trent lowered his head. He picked up the guard, cradling him like an oversized infant. With faltering steps, he approached the uncovered manhole. He stood for a moment, the tips of his toes hanging out over the edge; then he dangled the officer headfirst above the gaping darkness – and let go.

One light *thunk* marked the collision between body and ladder, which was followed three seconds later by a conclusive, echoey crunch as the body hit the ground, flesh popping and bones snapping.

Trenton pulled off his backpack, which had stayed secure against his back throughout the fight with the guard. He extracted a folder and began posting the same material around the PTS station. Blondy stood there, staring at the hole down which the guard had disappeared only moments ago.

Trenton didn't press her to help. Working as quickly as he could, he shoved his mind away from everything besides the task at hand. He was in the middle of posting his fifth flier when she jolted herself into action and joined him. Together, they finished with the station. In all, it took less than fifteen minutes.

Thinking of the body at the bottom of the ladder, Trent asked for the flashlight, and took the lead on the way down for the first time[1].

---

[1] Damn right.

The semi-hypnotic descent into the tunnel system left Trenton in a daze as he scanned the ground for the guard's body. Blondy was still only halfway down the ladder, knowing what waited at the bottom.

The beam of light found a booted foot first, and Trenton slowly raised the flashlight, having to be certain of what he already knew. The light reached what remained of the man's head and any fears that he had survived the fall were put to rest. *Good,* Trenton thought. And promptly threw up.

The girl was finally nearing the ground so Trent backtracked the few feet to the ladder. "Which way's the last station?" he asked.

"Hold on." She took out her map, deliberated, then pointed to a tunnel. "That's the one we want." Needless to say, it went right past the fresh corpse of the guard. Trent held on to the flashlight and grabbed ahold of Blondy, doing his best to illuminate the way ahead without alighting on the grizzly scene near their feet. For the most part he succeeded, but the squish under his right shoe was undoubtedly some sort of bodily fluid. As to whether it was his own or the unfortunate guard's, that was a mystery he'd rather not unravel.

"Hey, you think you can trust me with your name yet? I'm getting kind of tired of calling you Blondy in my head," Trent said, partly for the given reason but mostly for a distraction of any kind.

"That's what you've been calling me? Really stretched your brain on that one." The silence stretched out for an unspecified amount of time and Trent had nearly given up hope for a distraction when she said, "Beth. My name's Beth. And I already know you're Trenton."

"How do you know that? I thought the Resistance was extra secretive about that kind of stuff."

"They are. But for whatever reason, you're the only one from inside the city who they've made one of their own. They even gave you a type of invisibility from The Program, though they won't tell anyone else how yours works. Only a few of us know about you, but I'm one of them."

By this point they had safely passed any remnants of the body (and Trent's vomit) and were nearing the final PTS station. "Who knew I was so popular." Trent was trying for a joke, but in the aftermath of the last few hours, it came off as more of a listless observation.

The last ladder of the night[1] appeared in front of them and they climbed quickly to the top. Trenton was once more in the lead and he carefully taped the final disk to the underside of the manhole door and twisted the hatch open.

He heard and saw no one, so he slid out of the hole and helped Beth up after him.

Trenton looked over at her when they had finished putting up the last of the fliers, not sure what to say. So he turned and headed home.

[1] Trenton wouldn't be disappointed if it turned out to be the last ladder of his life

CHAPTER TWENTY-THREE

Trent was still groggy from the night before; he could barely keep his eyes open as he walked back to the PTS station he had come from not three hours ago. People hurried around him on their way to work and guards eyed them all, expressions inscrutable. *Please still be there,* Trenton thought. He drew near the station and felt his stomach clench up in anticipation.

Stepping into the main room of the station, Trenton was confronted with a throng of immobile bodies and hushed voices. The walls of the room were still plastered with photos and stories about the six victims of the Trials and – for the time being at least – there were no guards in sight. Some people were examining the entire room before moving on to a Pod, while others only looked at a few posters, but everyone took at least a moment to learn more about the victims.

As the crowd slowly shuffled forward, it remained constant in size; those leaving were replaced by fresh faces at the entrance to the station. There was a good chance Trenton and the others around him would be late for work[1], but he couldn't bring himself to care. Instead he looked around at the posters closest to him as he edged towards a pod. He'd spent all night putting up these fliers, but staring at them now, grief surged through him. He saw normal people, surrounded by their families, playing with their children, posing with coworkers, celebrating birthdays. Looking around at his fellow commuters, he could picture any one of them up on the wall alongside the other victims. He only hoped that the lives of these six ordinary people, thrown into chaos and disaster, might force these people to reexamine how their city was run. Maybe it would be enough to turn the people against the government and The

---

[1] If the rest of the stations were in a similar state, then most of the city would be late as well.

Program. Maybe when the time came to set the last part of the plan in motion, the Resistance wouldn't be fighting alone.

He was broken out of his reverie by the jostling of a neighbor who pointed out that he had reached the end of the station. Resuming his slow shuffle forward, he tapped his ring and stepped into the mouth of a waiting pod.

After the pod arrived outside the Schools, Trenton exited the station and walked out into the day. He had only made it a few feet when two guards pushed past him and descended into the station; the posters wouldn't be up for much longer. Trent bubbled up with laughter. It was too late – virtually every commuter must have seen the memorials by now, and they would tell anyone who hadn't. Trenton was curious how the government would react. Would they rush to take it all down (which would take hours) or would they leave it up and flood the news with reports of how it was all lies.

He kept walking to his building instead of following the guards back down; most everyone was rushing to work or school and he didn't want to stand out in the crowd. He was already five minutes late, but he was sure he wasn't the only one. On his way to his classroom he saw four other teachers hurrying to their respective rooms, confirming this thought.

When he reached his class, every student was accounted for, save one. The schools still made use of buses, which wouldn't have been affected by the clogged PTS stations. The one missing student was most likely home sick. Every teacher knows how rare it is to have every student present at the same time.

Trenton proceeded to lecture for the following fifty-eight minutes, all the while itching to know how the government was reacting to the memorials. There was a five-minute break as the students switched out, and Trenton resumed lecturing, this time for an hour and five minutes. (He had shown up more than five minutes late in the first class if you remember. You should, it was only two paragraphs ago.)

Eventually, the last bell rang and Trenton fought to restrain himself from tearing out of the classroom. The students slowly disappeared out the door while Trenton graded assignments and finished whatever other thrilling work teachers do.

He sat at his desk for another half hour, then left, sure to shut off the lights and lock the door as he went. Entering the PTS station, he noted the clean white walls of the room before accessing a pod and taking a seat

They must have waited for most people to get to work and then cleaned them all up as fast as they could, Trenton thought from his seat in the pod. *Too bad people won't be cleansed of what they've learned as easily as the walls of the stations.*

He made it back home and turned on the news to find out how the government was going to explain away the information and images that had covered those walls.

The Newswoman was in the middle of discussing the latest episodes of The Program, something they did when there wasn't enough real news to go around. Which was most days. But today *wasn't* one of those days. Trenton had been in one of the PTS stations this morning. He had seen how people had reacted. This was *not* nothing.

Trent's head was beginning to buzz from his growing irritation, but he kept the news on, waiting for the memorials to be mentioned. Finally, 41 minutes and 1 second into Trenton's news binge, the "petty vandalism of the Public Transport System" received a passing mention. Supposedly, the perpetrators – all teenagers playing a prank – were already caught.

The news cycle soon began anew, and Trenton heard nothing more about this morning's "petty vandalism" before he shut off the H-display in disgust.

Not feeling up to cooking, he ordered delivery from a nearby Italian bistro: spaghetti and meatballs. Next, he messaged Jess, asking how she was doing. He got a quick reply back that she was doing better than the last time they had spoken, during the week of Trials for the government murders.

"That's good," Trenton typed back. "We should get together soon and talk."

"K. Maybe sometime in the next few days."

At this moment, Trent's ring pinged, alerting him that his food had arrived. He opened the apartment door, paid with his ring, and rushed into the kitchen to begin chomping down.

∎▪▪▪∎

A week passed, and like most of life had been until recently, it was drearily uneventful. School would soon come to an end, leaving Trenton with even more time to do nothing of interest. He hadn't yet heard from the Resistance, but he was curious about how they had interpreted the government's reaction to the memorials.

Saturday night came and Trenton considered heading to the bar, but decided to wait another week, in case the government was still riled up. Fighting off boredom (and the anxiety of the unknown), he spent the night exploring an alien planet through the wonders of virtual reality. He became so engrossed in the false world around him that it was nearly midnight when he shut it off and prepared for bed. He was three quarters of the way done brushing his teeth when he heard a soft creak from somewhere outside his bedroom. *This again?* He looked to his ring on the bedside table, but it slept on peacefully, unaware of any late-night intruders.

Trenton finished with his teeth and crept out into the living room. Faced with an empty room, he relaxed marginally, but moved to check the kitchen. Inside, he encountered a rather unexpected sight. The medium-sized backside of Savior Jim protruded from the fridge, an array of (Trenton's) snacks already splayed out on the counter.

"The Resistance not feeding you enough?" Trenton asked.

Without moving from his position in the fridge, Jim replied, "Sneaking around is hard work. Sometimes you need a little midnight snack to refuel."

"Uhuh. Do you have something to say to me or are you just here for the free food?"

Jim turned around indignantly[1], cradling an assortment of fruit, cheeses, and yogurts. "Actually I do have something to say to you." He set down the food in a pile next to the rest of his plunder. "I'm sure you've noticed the government's reaction to our memorials in the PTS stations. And by that I mean their complete lack of reaction."

Trent nodded.

"It means we're finally getting to them. They realize that they can't crucify innocent people to punish us, because that backfired on them, and if they make a big deal about the stations, it'll seem like they're just trying to cover it up."

"So you're trying to tell me it's good that they've ignored it?"

---

[1] Trenton had no idea how the man managed to make a simple turn of the body portray his indignance, but that was exactly what he did.

"Yes and no. They're *very* pissed off and they won't underestimate us again. But from what we've learned from spying on The Program, it seems like people were really affected by even a brief view of those posters. I've been told it was your idea to honor the victims as a way of gathering support to overthrow the government. Not to mention the guard you took care of down in the tunnels. Great job."

Trenton barely noticed the praise. "Thanks. So does this mean you're going to clue me in on the last part of the plan?"

"Yes, I think you've earned a place in the final push," Jim said, and proceeded to explain the details of the plan. Trenton had been left in the dark for so long that he kept waiting for Savior Jim to laugh and say, "Just kidding! That's not the plan *at all.*" But that moment never came. When Jim finished speaking, Trent was left to contemplate the effects his actions – along with the rest of the Resistance's –would have on the people of this city.

Jim let him roll the plan over in his mind, then broke the silence. "So what do you think?"

"Sounds risky as hell. And people will die on both sides. But fuck it, it might actually work."

CHAPTER TWENTY-FOUR

A month passed and summer began in earnest. School ended, leaving Trent with a surplus of time to ponder the implications of the Resistance's plan. He felt like he was missing something – was there a flaw in the plan? Or was it something else? His mind felt foggy most of the time, which didn't help. He was waiting for the day when he could finally put this uncertain limbo behind him.

Fortunately, that day was fast approaching. Soon enough, everything would be decided, and you, the persistent reader, will finally be able to discard this novel once and for all.

And so we begin the end.

Trenton lounged in his usual chair in front of the H-display. To the ever-watching outside eyes, the day appeared no different than any other in recent memory. Dusk was settling upon the city and people who actually worked during the summer[1] were arriving home to watch some of The Program before having dinner with their family. Children came home from friends' houses, or from playing outside, or from the sanctuary of their own room where they had been absorbed all day in the virtues of virtual reality.

The usual primetime shows were on; Trenton was enduring an episode of "The Streets" where a massive gang fight was about to take place (ok he was loving it).

The fight was just getting underway when the screen shuddered[2] and went black. 3.4 seconds later a new image appeared on the holographic display. It was the one and only Savior Jim, his face grave as he stared through the screen, and seemingly right into Trent's living room.

---

[1] That clearly didn't include Trenton. Oh the perks of being a teacher.

[2] An admittedly odd thing for a screen to do.

"This is the Resistance. We are preparing to overthrow the government and dismantle The Program. Remember those who have been tortured, imprisoned, murdered for saying one word the government didn't approve of. Without the Program in place, you and your family could speak freely, could be truly alone at last." Jim paused here for three seconds. "For any unwilling or unable to help, please remain in the safety of your homes. Any who wish to help, to be truly free, join us in the streets now to end this once and for all."

The screen went black again, every few minutes repeating the same message for any who missed it. Trent lurched out of his chair and ran to his bedroom. He pulled open his sock drawer and retrieved the coin that would render him invisible to The Program. Next, he flew to his closet, diving down to find the gun – no silencer this time – that Savior Jim had given him at the end of his last visit.

He turned off the safety and turned to look out his bedside window. The streets were nearly empty besides the guards who roamed around, now severely agitated. *They must have heard the good news,* Trenton thought with a hint of a grin. But where were the ordinary people fighting back? Were they too frightened to help?

Trenton waited at the window, praying for someone to be brave enough to fight. Without the chaos and distraction their help would afford, there was no way Trenton – or any of the other Resistance members – would be able to reach the control stations of The Program.

As the minutes passed by, Trent's hope began to fade. If nothing happened soon, the Resistance was doomed. Then he noticed a blur of activity in the lobby of the building across the street. A closer look revealed a group of people talking, preparing to venture out into the street. Trenton examined other nearby buildings and saw the same thing in almost every one. A blink of an eye later, and the groups started pouring out of the buildings, charging at any guards in sight.

"Fuck *yes!*" Trenton yelled as he rushed to leave his apartment. He sped down the stairs and out into the street.

The guards began firing into the crowd, downing a significant portion of the mob. But the crowd resisted, wielding broken chair legs, kitchen knives, or their bare fists. There were too many of them for the guards to hold off at a distance, and they were quickly drawn into close-quarter fights, being beaten or stabbed until they fell to the ground. Even once on the ground, the incited rioters continued to tear at the bodies until the less blood-crazed members of the group pulled them off to search for other, more lively threats. They left nine bodies on the ground behind them, either completely still or in their last spasms, surrounded by a growing pool of blood.

Trent had been standing near the entrance to his building, frozen by the turmoil on every side of him, but the death of the last few nearby guards reminded him of his task. With a fevered shake of his head, he started running down the street, doing his best to avoid both the mob and any guards. He kept his gun tucked under the back of his shirt, thinking it would be easier to move around if he didn't appear to be a threat.

He made it three blocks before he was stopped by a frantic guard. The man pointed a gun at Trenton's chest from where he stood, just ten feet away. "Don't move! I *will* shoot you."

Slowly, Trenton raised his hands into the air. "Ok, I'm not moving. Can you tell me what's going on?"

"You don't know? The Resistance is attacking. They've even hijacked The Program," the guard said, sounding close to panic.

Trenton started to shuffle towards the guard, trying to get close enough to have a chance at taking him down. "Stop! Stop moving!" Trent kept inching towards the guard. He was now only four feet from the barrel of the gun. He saw the guard's finger twitch over the trigger, and prepared to launch himself forward. Suddenly, a yell burst into the air, seemingly from the direction Trent had just come. The guard reflexively glanced in the direction of the sound, and Trenton tackled him to the ground. They fought for control of the gun, but the man was far stronger than Trenton and quickly gained the upper hand. He rolled over onto Trenton and began to pry the gun from his fingers. He wrenched it free and smashed Trent's face with the butt of the pistol, breaking his nose[1] and causing a gush of blood to run down into his mouth.

The guard was swearing at him, cursing him for trying to survive. What a damned fool thing to do.

Trenton watched the gun rise up again through squinting, bleary eyes. Watched as the barrel pointed at his head, unable to move under the crushing weight of the officer, hearing nothing over the dull roar that inexplicably filled his ears. He waited for the bullet, wondering if he would hear the explosion as it left the barrel of the gun, if the sound of it

---

[1] It was obvious from sharp pain he felt, the crunch, and the difficulty he had getting a full breath.

would pierce his stubborn eardrums, or if the world would simply turn black.

Then a sharp crack broke through the haze and Trenton turned his head back and forth, trying to determine the source of the sound. He figured it wasn't the gun against his head, since he was still alive[1]. And anyways, that wasn't how a gun was supposed to sound. A moment later, the heavy weight pressing him into the ground dissolved, leaving only the throb of his nose behind. He lifted his head up, pretty damn curious about 1: why he was alive, 2: what had happened to the guard, and 3: if whatever had happened to the guard was about to happen to him.

Standing around him were three teenagers, carrying an assortment of scrounged-together weapons. Their mouths were moving and they looked somewhat concerned. When he didn't respond to their questions[2], they moved to lift him up, and the sudden change in elevation did wonders for his hearing. He even managed to form a few words. "I need to get to the Screens." They came out nasally and slow, but they were definitely words.

The two boys holding him up exchanged glances, with the girl keeping watch. It was the girl who finally answered. "Good luck then. That's the craziest part of the city from what we hear. We want to help fight the government but we're not stupid. You go there and the odds are you're gonna die."

Trenton didn't bother replying, just started walking in the direction he supposed the Screens were (he was a little disoriented). The two boys kept hold of him, keeping him from falling, and the one on Trent's left said, "I guess we can stay with you for a couple blocks. Maybe by then you'll have recovered a little more." The other two nodded their agreement.

Together, they walked towards the Screens, slowly at first. After a few minutes, Trenton's strength returned and they began to move more quickly.

The blond-haired boy on Trent's right spoke for the first time. "Why don't we just take you to a PTS station? You'd get there much faster and have less chance of being shot."

---

[1] He was pretty sure he was alive, but not a full 100%. More like 89%.

[2] Well he imagined they were questions. Its difficult to know for sure when all you hear is some garbled nonsense as if through a dense fog.

The girl continued scanning the street as she thought it over. There were a few scuffles taking place ahead and behind them, but nothing too worrying. "With everything going on, it's probably not running. And if it is, they might try stopping it if someone they see as a threat gets on it." She swept her gaze over Trent's broken nose. "Not that you look like much of a threat."

"That's exactly why I didn't head there in the first place," Trenton said, pointedly ignoring her last comment. The two boys had released him a minute ago but still stood close by on either side.

They rounded a corner and ran into a wall of smoke. Trenton placed the crook of his arm over his face to protect his lungs and exhaled sharply at the surge of pain in his nose. His eyes stung as he forced them open and tried to inspect their new surroundings, but the smoke hid anything more than a couple feet away.

His three young protectors gathered around him, alert for an ambush as they shuffled through the smog. Trenton gestured to the wall of buildings on their right and said. "Stay close to the buildings. It'll keep us from going in circles and limit the directions an attack could come from." His voice was muffled by the sleeve of his shirt (which he now held very gingerly over his nose), but his companions seemed to understand.

Within a matter of three steps, the temperature seemed to rise exponentially. Trenton wiped a film of sweat from his forehead with his free hand, but a new layer sprang up within seconds. The others were similarly affected, though they kept moving without a word. Trent searched for the source of the heat and smoke, but needn't have bothered: Through the haze, tall flames of bright red and orange became visible, licking up the side of the next building on their right. The heat became unbearable, forcing the group to circle around the burning building. They used the still visible fire as their guide until they passed the conflagration and were able to return to the row of buildings.

The heat at their backs pushed them forward until the smoke started to thin. As the smoke dissipated, Trent was able to examine their surroundings in detail, which was both a relief and a shock. The four of them looked around the street. There was not a single living body in sight, but their stomachs turned over at the dozen or so bodies that lay unmoving on the hard gray ground, broken and bloody.

Trenton walked resolutely forward, doing his best to ignore the motionless guards and rioters who lay side by side, united in death. His new friends weren't so callous; they were visibly shaken by the death that hovered at their feet and Trenton was reminded just how young they were. Not to mention they had met less than thirty minutes ago. For some reason these three kids, none of whom looked to be older than seventeen, had committed to helping him without knowing who he was or what he was trying to do.

They had already come more than the couple of blocks they had promised and showed no signs of abandoning him yet. "Is there a reason you're helping me?" He said with a glance at each of them. "I'm not a hero if that's what you're imagining. I've done some horrible things."

"But you're part of the Resistance," the girl stated.

"And you know that because..."

"You're carrying a gun – I saw it in the back of your shirt before – and you were fighting a guard by yourself. Plus, this whole thing doesn't seem to faze you in the least. It's like you knew it was coming. I seriously doubt the government knew about this ahead of time or they would have done something to stop it. That only leaves one option: you're a member of the Resistance."

Trenton raised an eyebrow at her. "Ok, I'm slightly impressed. I would ask your name, but I don't want to put you in any more danger than you already are."

"It's Rebecca."

Looking at the boys on either side of him, Trent said, "And what about you two? Are you just along for the ride?"

"We're her friends. And we trust her instincts," said the boy on Trent's left, pushing his unruly dark hair out of his eyes to give Trenton a suitably defiant stare.

By this point they had escaped any sign of the fire, but Trenton glimpsed through the cracks between skyscrapers and noticed several more clouds of smoke rising up into the sky; they were materializing all around the city. "We're only four blocks away from the Screens," Trent said. "Maybe you guys should clear out."

The three shared a glance and the boy on Trenton's left spoke up again. "We'll take you a little farther."

"I really have to learn that trick. I've never been too good at telepathy," Trent said. His nose had stopped bleeding but if he looked down, he could just make out the squashed mess it had become.

The closer they drew to the Screens, the more violent the road ahead of them became. Guards shot into throngs of angry citizens, who charged any symbol of the government with a ferocious intensity. The three teenagers and Trenton navigated the treacherous obstacle course of bodies and gunfire. They fought only when forced to, instead focusing all their energy on getting as close to the Screens as possible.

Trenton's pistol still hid in the back of his shirt, tucked into his jeans. He had only six shots; he had to make them count.

They took a side street into the Screens plaza in the hope of avoiding the bulk of the fighting. There *were* far fewer skirmishes in the narrow alley, but the way was not entirely clear. An otherwise unoccupied guard challenged them at the entrance to the plaza, his gun pointed at the ground in front of them. Clearly he didn't see them as much of a threat.

Without hesitation, Rebecca sprinted at the officer and before he could even raise his gun, she whipped her metal pipe into his head. The man collapsed with a thud that declared him either dead or thoroughly unconscious. Needless to say, they didn't stop to check which.

The inside of the plaza was blanketed in a thin layer of shadows. The sun had nearly set and the enclosing buildings blocked out most of the remaining light. The four giant screens were dark. Only a few scattered people fought inside – the open space coupled with the high walls made it an ideal place to be taken out by gunfire.

Trenton stopped at the edge of the square and turned to his young bodyguards. "Okay, you've taken me far enough, and saved my life more than a few times on the way. You should really leave. Go back home and wait this out."

"Fuck that. We're not sitting at home while our city's future hangs in the balance." It was the boy from Trenton's right, who had barely spoken until this point.

After a second, Rebecca nodded and the boy on Trent's left followed suit.

Trent breathed out a harsh, raspy breath and stepped back from the three of them. He yanked out his gun and leveled it at chest height.

He swiveled it back and forth between the three teenagers. "You're going to slowly circle around me, leave the square, and keep walking until you're out of my sight. And then you can do whatever you want, though I would love it if you went back to your homes."

The dark haired boy was the first to find his tongue. "This is how you pay us back? By pointing a gun at us?"

Rebecca placed a hand on the boy's shoulder. "Come on, getting him mad at us isn't going to help anything." She guided the two boys, practically pushing them around Trenton and out of the plaza.

Trent waited until they had disappeared from sight, then returned his gun to the back of his pants and reassessed the state of the square. There were three guards fighting a group of five men off to his left. Aside from that, the plaza was empty.

He pinpointed the door he had entered all those months ago when the government had "convinced" him to stop teaching the virtues of a world without The Program. The memory of the hundreds of brightly lit monitors playing back the lives of the entire city was seared into his brain. The door was nearly straight across the square from where he stood, and walking directly towards it would bring him uncomfortably close to the fighting.

Trenton started moving on a diagonal, away from the violence, but in the general direction of the door. He kept his eyes on the ground and moved slowly, trying to avoid drawing attention to himself.

He was near the center of the plaza when two of the protesters fell, dead. The other three fought with renewed anger, but the odds were now stacked against them. It may have been three against three, but the guards' training and superior weapons allowed them to quickly gain the upper hand.

Fearing the last of the protesters would be killed before he made it to the door, Trenton hurried his pace. So far he had remained unnoticed by the guards, but that could change in an instant. His heart ricocheted around inside his chest, the door never getting any closer as he jerked his head back and forth between it and the ongoing battle to his left.

And then he was inside. Inside the white hallway without doors, where he had walked with that mysterious man, worried for the safety of his uneventful life close to a year ago. He had no recollection of opening the door to the building. Shouldn't it have been locked? No, he remembered the outer door opening without issue. *It's the door at the end of the hallway that's going to require some thinking*, he remembered, picturing the government agent placing his palm against the wall.

How the hell was he going to get through that? He strode to the end of the hallway as if he had any clue what he was doing. When he reached the white wall, he stopped and looked for anything out of the ordinary. He found nothing. Feeling silly, he raised his right hand and pressed it, palm forward, onto the wall. He kept his palm to the wall and waited, but of course nothing happened. Unsurprised but disappointed, Trent let his hand fall from the smooth plaster – and a second later, the entire wall slid open.

How...? Maybe the Resistance was able to turn off the security protocols? He shook his head and didn't waste any more time questioning it, pulling out his pistol and scanning the inside of the room. Aisles of computers filled the room, like he remembered; they were chest height with about six inches between them, making it difficult but not impossible to hide behind them. Most of the screens were black, and those that were on showed only various menus and settings. He didn't see anyone in front of any of the screens or crouched down behind them, and at first Trenton thought they had all fled. Then he noticed the group of people huddled in the corner of the room.

He checked the rest of the room quickly while keeping one eye on the corner containing the panic-stricken workers. He was entering the second to last aisle when he heard light footsteps running towards him. With surprising[1] speed, he spun around, aimed at the charging man, and shot him once in the chest. The man kept coming but now he was stumbling the last few feet. Not wanting to waste another bullet, Trenton kicked him in the stomach, throwing the man onto his back where he lay gasping and shuddering.

"Anyone else want to try that?" Trenton asked, looking towards the corner where the rest of the people were clustered. Nobody made a sound. "Didn't think so."

Trenton walked closer to the group of people until he was about ten feet away. There appeared to be around twenty of them in all. He held the gun firmly in his hand, pointed halfway between the closest body and the ground directly below. "Now you're going to tell me who's in charge of this station or I'm going to start shooting you all, one by one."

---

[1] He even surprised himself.

Still no one spoke, so Trenton raised his gun the rest of the way. He meticulously shifted from person to person until he settled on a middle-aged woman near the front. "This woman dies if you don't tell me who's in charge in five seconds. And if you try lying to me, I'll kill you two by two instead."

The woman was noticeably trembling but Trenton kept his face a mask of indifference. He cocked the gun – and the woman looked to her right, to a balding man who refused to return her gaze. "Is that him?" Trenton asked. The woman froze. Trent shot her in the head. She collapsed, and the man behind her whimpered.

He had only four bullets left now. Trenton raised his gun to the man who had whimpered; sweat had started to drip down the man's set of chins. "Who's in charge? If you tell me, I promise I'll let you live."

The man squeezed his eyes shut. Trenton prodded him with the end of the pistol, causing him to jump into the air and his eyes to snap open. With a dripping sausage of a finger, he pointed to the same balding man the first woman had looked to.

"Thank you." Trenton moved to the leader of the station. "Get up." The man struggled to gain his feet. Trent led him to a nearby monitor at gunpoint. "I want you to turn off the distress signal you initiated when the government lost control of The Program."

The man started typing as Trenton added, "If you don't disable it, or you try warning the government, the others I'm working with will know. Then they'll let me know, and I'll let *you* know by shooting everyone in this room while you watch, then shooting you in both kneecaps and letting you bleed out."

The man paled, then nodded and returned to his work, with Trenton watching over his shoulder, periodically turning to ensure the other workers were still suitably cowed.

The leader of the station stepped back from the monitor and looked to Trenton. "Okay. It's done."

Trenton tuned a monitor to a random channel of The Program. "And now we wait. Once all the other control stations have been taken, the Resistance will send out a broadcast using The Program."

And so they waited.

The screen was blank for another forty minutes before it flickered twice and the face of Savior Jim appeared on the screen.

"We have successfully taken control of every station monitoring The Program and disabled them. We will permanently destroy each station over the next few hours, and take into custody anyone involved. Thanks to you all, this city is free for the first time in over twenty years." He smiled into the camera. "Any guards still fighting are encouraged to lay down their weapons and surrender. We will not harm anyone who was a part of the old government so long as they cooperate.

"All citizens are asked to return to their homes after the remaining guards surrender. Communications through your rings are still down, as they are connected to The Program. We will restore them as soon as we are able. Thank you."

Minutes later, Savior Jim himself stepped into the room, along with three other members of the Resistance. Trenton looked for the explosives the Resistance would use to destroy the station, but didn't see them.

"There's been a change in the plan," Jim said in response to Trent's stare, his face hard as concrete. "We're going to preserve the stations in case they're needed in the future."

"Why would they ever be needed? The whole point of this was to get rid of them so that The Program would be completely destroyed." Trenton still had his gun in hand.

Savior Jim didn't reply. Just turned to the man Trenton had singled out as the leader of the group. "You'll remain in charge here as long as you can cooperate."

Jim's guards had approached Trenton as Savior Jim was talking, and now they pried the gun from his frozen fingers. Two of them stood by him with their pistols pointed in his direction as the head of the station nodded mutely.

"Just to be perfectly clear, *no one* learns that The Program will continue to exist. Anyone who even hints at it will be… taken care of."

Trenton could hardly contain his frustration. "And how the fuck are you going to hide it? I think people will notice when they see themselves and people they know showing up on TV again."

Savior glanced at Trent. "People *won't* be showing up on TV. At least not *here*. The Program will stop broadcasting the footage it captures inside the city and we will dismantle the existing cameras – they're ancient anyway. We're going to insert cameras so small they can't be seen. And of course we'll still be watching through your rings. Imagine how much happier everyone will be, thinking they've finally regained their privacy, and how much more uninhibited they will be. We'll have better footage and a better city. We'll sell The Program to the rest of the world instead of broadcasting anything locally, increasing our audience one-hundredfold."

Without warning, a barrage of gunshots ricocheted off walls and buried into bodies; Trenton was too overwhelmed to do anything more than remain standing. The three guards still leveled their guns in the air, but nearly every government employee had already collapsed. Only the head official, Trenton, and the four members of the Resistance had remained unscathed.

"What the fuck!" Trenton screamed, mostly out of rage and disgust, but also because he couldn't hear for shit.

Jim yelled calmly back at him. "Now there's only one person left at every station, and far less chance of anyone letting anything slip. And if they do, they'll be taken care of immediately. Not to mention the fact that a few "crackpots" won't be able to convince an entire city of something completely ridiculous."

The guards had seized hold of Trenton after his last outburst and he fought to break free with all his moderately substantial might. Getting nowhere, he stopped struggling. "Motherfucker. I know your city is in trouble, but what about trading with us, and taking half or even all of our resources. This is sadistic."

Savior Jim's iron expression softened for a second. "It's not. It's what we have to do to survive. We hoped we could follow through with our original plan. But all the government's money has been going straight back into the city, and there's barely any stored up at all. Trade alone won't be enough to save our city – in the year it's taken to finish this revolution, things have gotten even worse. I'm sorry, but it's us or you, and honestly, if they don't know they're being watched and recorded then what's the difference?"

Trenton considered spitting in his face, but decided he'd rather live a little while longer. Jim gave him one final stare, then waved to the guards to let him go. "You can see yourself out."

Trenton walked, head bowed, towards the exit. He knew there was nothing he could do, that no one would believe him, and it infuriated him. He was battered by the knowledge that all the work he had done these past few months was meaningless. But worst of all, he was suddenly horrified by the deaths he personally had caused, thinking it would lead to better lives for the city as a whole. Now he was nothing more than a murderer. *Well*, he thought. *I guess I was a murderer before too.*

He walked out into night, filled with hatred. In the darkness, the dim wavering of distant fires was easily visible. The sounds of jubilant celebrations echoed in his eardrums. On his path through the city, he strolled past motionless bodies, of which there were far too many to count. He carried no light of his own, finding his way only by the ambient light of the burning buildings. On the dark gray ground were the darker stains of bodily fluids of all kinds.

The occasional screams of those still fighting floated through the air, creating a fitting soundtrack when overlayed with the rhythmic shouts of revelry. Destruction was just a step away from euphoria after all. He was still reeling from the immensity of the betrayal. His stomach was sick with it. He urged his body to move faster, to run, but he continued on at the same plodding pace, unable to leave behind the cruel, inevitable world that made its home around him.

Everything he and the people of this city had done to earn their right to privacy was worthless. And now no one even knew they were being watched. It was a far more insidious evil. People would go about their lives thinking they were free, unaware of the now invisible eyes of the government, watching and recording their most intimate moments.

Maybe ignorance is bliss, Trent thought as he wandered through the streets. *Either way, I don't want to be a part of it.* For the first time, Trenton considered leaving the city as more than an impossible dream. Not because it was any less impossible (although it probably was, currently), but because he wasn't sure he could live the rest of his life knowing what everyone else did not. That their lives were still being watched, recorded, and sold for a tidy profit. And he was partially to blame.

Trenton remembered the coin in his pocket and pulled it out. He examined both of its faces in the red-orange light of the persisting fires. In that instant, he made up his mind. He hurled the coin away from him, losing it in the blackness of the night. He turned in (what he believed to be) the direction of his apartment and strode purposefully towards it.

He had traveled only a few more steps when a group of revelers burst out of a nearby building. They moved into Trenton's path, shouting and singing (horribly). Trent shifted to the side of the street without breaking his stride and passed them by. One or two yelled catcalls at his back but he refused to acknowledge them.

More and more figures were piling into the streets around him to join in the celebrations, slowing his progress. He mercilessly pushed his way through the thickening crowd, some of whom pushed back. Nonetheless, he eventually arrived back at his building. He climbed the three flights of stairs to his apartment, and stepped inside.

Looking around his small apartment, he was caught off guard by how ordinary it appeared. It looked no different then it had when he had left earlier that evening. No bodies lay sprawled on the ground, no flames dined on the rugs and furniture[1]. Taking a plus-sized breath, Trent moved farther into the living room. He looked around at his meager possessions, most of which could have belonged to anyone.

His fingers traced the virtual display that cycled steadily between a small selection of photos of Trent with Jessica, Jason, and one or two with Molly (which he had been unable to delete). In his closet he found his hiking backpack that he used when rock-climbing. He stuffed in three sets of clothes, and looked to his ring, which he had left on his bedside table before heading out before. He left it where it lay.

Moving to the kitchen, he extracted the small amount of food that could last in the summer heat. Then he filled up two water bottles – the only two he owned – with water. The virtual clock in the corner claimed pompously that it was only 11pm. *Bullshit.*

Trent racked his brain for anything he was forgetting. A flashlight might have been nice, but he'd always had his ring for light, and old-fashioned flashlights were uncommon. Before he left he took a quick shower and threw on his set of black clothes. The same clothes he had worn the night he had killed a government official. The same clothes from the night he had helped decorate the PTS stations as memorials for the six victims, and murdered a guard.

Bag packed and body clean(er), Trenton looked around his apartment for a final time, and walked out into the hallway, the door closing shut with an ill-fitting *woosh*.

When he stepped out into the night, he was met with a tepid breeze, newly-developed since his walk home. Throngs of people still filled the sidewalks and the streets. They weren't doing much of anything except getting in Trenton's way, and he was getting tired of their misplaced exuberance.

---

[1] This was theoretically possible considering the number of fires that had popped up around the city.

Even so, he made it to the edge of the crowd – they were clustered in the more densely populated areas of the city, which was of course where Trenton lived – without any serious incidents. No one tried stopping him; he probably looked to be just another happy face. (That was sarcasm).

As he drew closer to the farmland that encircled the city, he made good use of back alleys and stayed within the shadows as much as possible. If they were already making use of The Program, they wouldn't have too much difficulty concluding he was trying to leave the city and tracking him the whole way. He was counting on the chaos of the night to be enough to allow him to escape, but he had no delusions about his chances.

Looking out from the shadows of the last layer of buildings, Trenton assessed the situation. There was no fence to mark the edge of the city limits, since anyone trying to escape would be shot down long before they cleared the mile-wide region of farms and forests. Trenton had intentionally picked a place that was almost half forest. Out on the open fields he would be easily seen and killed; he figured his best chance was under the cover of trees.

Setting his sights on the nearest swath of forest, he sprinted out of the city and into the field of close-cropped vegetation. He didn't look around, knowing if someone was there to shoot him, he was already dead. The pounding of his shoes on unknown vegetation matched his pulsing heartbeat. One moment he was fully expecting to be shot, and the next he was "safely" inside the forest.

He had never been in this part of the farm region. He had considered taking the route where he had gone rock-climbing at the very beginning of this story, but he figured the new government would have access to all the old footage, and would know he had been out that way before.

Now that he was fully ensconced within the forest, the darkness was absolute; neither the light from the three-quarter-moon nor the bleeding remnants of light from the city were able to shove their way through the clusters of leaves and branches. Without a flashlight to light his way, Trenton stumbled blindly through the dense copse of trees. He reached his hands out in front of him and moved at a speed of inches per hour. The forest was full of rustling branches and the light pawsteps of unseen animals. He strained to hear any sounds of pursuit, but they were either masked by the forest or didn't exist at all.

Soon the adrenaline began to fade, and Trenton was engulfed by a pervasive exhaustion and a savory blend of fears. Fears that were only a step away from becoming reality. The most pressing fear was that he was being followed, or that he would emerge from the forest only to be shot and killed. Coming in right behind at number two on the list was the fear that he was going in circles and would waste the rest of the night (or longer) searching for a way out. This scenario would either end with the new government killing him while he was still lost or with him getting captured when he finally found his way outside. And then killed.

Trenton steered his attention back to his immediate problem – carefully moving forward and listening for any signs of danger. Ironically, this was the exact moment that his foot caught on a protruding root, compromising his balance. He stifled a cry of shock as he tumbled to the ground. His brief shout seemed impossibly loud in the imprint of his mind as he lay in a heap on the forest floor, frozen, listening for any sound of renewed pursuit. When nothing penetrated the usual soundscape of the forest, Trenton climbed to his feet and resumed his awkward march through the trees.

What felt like hours passed by and still Trent shuffled onwards, unaware of any possible changes taking place around him in the suffocating blackness, only certain that the trees still rustled and the animals still prowled about. He settled into a daze, his mind pushing his body onward but doing little else.

At some point he stumbled, almost falling once again. But this time there was no root; the ground had subtly changed under his feet. Loose dirt, rocks, and the occasional root were replaced by *packed* dirt, rocks and roots. So all in all, not much of a change, but Trent wondered if he had found some sort of path. And if it was, was it still used? It didn't seem like the kind of thing the city's government would make use of, and he didn't have much chance of finding his way out of here without some sort of guide, so he decided to follow the feel of the path. It turned out to be much harder than anticipated. He had to backtrack more than once after noticing his feet were sinking farther into the ground, and really, have you ever tried following a path using only the feel of the ground on your feet? It's bloody difficult.

The one mercy was that the path barely curved at all, which kept Trenton from completely losing his way. He continued on in this manner, making progress towards what he hoped was the end of the trail and the edge of the forest.

Gradually, he began to identify the black shapes of tree trunks and branches and felt a surge of excitement. Above him, the darkness was as heavy as ever, indicating the light was filtering in through the lower levels of the forest – and that meant he was getting close. Close to… something… He had no idea what was this far from the heart of the city.

The pale moonlight grew stronger as the minutes ticked by, with Trenton progressing faster now that he was able to follow the trail by sight. He did his best to move quietly, for there were bound to be guards left at the border of the city's grounds. How many were there, and where were they stationed? Would there be an actual barrier blocking his way? That would complicate things just a little.

Finally, he reached the last line of trees. Trenton hugged the back of the tree closest to him and peered out into the night. The moon had reached its apex and begun its descent back towards the ground during the time Trenton had spent lost in the forest. It's light tainted Trent's view, giving everything a washed-out look. A solid concrete wall ringed with barbed wire at both the top and bottom was the first thing Trenton noticed. Next came the towers built into the wall at regular intervals. *What is this, a medieval siege wall? How the hell am I supposed to get past that?* Trent slid his gaze back and forth about the base of the wall and strained to see inside the nearest tower. The only visible door was closed, but a window yielded a partial view of the inside; he didn't see any guards within his limited view.

There must be at least one guy hiding in that tower, Trenton thought. *If I can somehow get over the wall without making noise, maybe I'll never even need to find out.* He snorted. Re-examining the wall, he judged it to be nearly thirty feet tall. He looked for any sign of a door that went straight through the wall, but as far as he could see in either direction (which admittedly wasn't too far in the sparse moonlight), there was no such thing.

For the first time since he had entered the forest, he thought of the cameras. There must be cameras all along the wall, but were they tied directly to The Program? The odds were good that they were.

Considering how far he had made it, he assumed they hadn't completely restarted The Program yet and would not be able to do much until then. It was possible that the guards were blind, except for what they could see with their own eyes. Either way, anyone remaining behind would be watching their respective areas as closely as they could; he had to assume that whenever he left the relative safety of the forest, any guards in the tower would attack.

Maybe something in the tower could help him get past the wall. But he had no weapon, no way to hide from the cameras. He'd have to charge the tower and catch anyone inside by surprise if he wanted to have any chance at all. Even then, he better be damn lucky.

No point waiting any longer, Trent decided, and lunged out from behind his tree. He rushed to the tower, reached the closed door, twisted the handle – but of course it was locked, a possibility he had somehow avoided considering. He had time for a single thought before a voice yelled at him through the door to stand back and keep his hands "where I can see 'em." That thought was, *What a moron.* He was referring to himself.

He stepped away from the door and raised his hands into the air. The door slammed open to reveal an absurdly muscular man, wielding an absurdly large gun.

"Is this a fucking joke?" Trenton asked. "They left one guy here, and it just happened to be you?"

Hulk[1] frowned slightly but kept the machine gun pointed at Trenton's chest. "Am I supposed to know you?" His voice was husky but oddly feminine and clashed jarringly with his appearance.

"No, it's just a big laugh that I thought I was so lucky they left only one or two guards here when the fighting started, but they left *you*, the biggest man I've ever seen, so I feel very *un*lucky now." Trent searched desperately for some way out of the (literal) crosshairs. "I bet you don't even know what happened back at the city."

When the man didn't react, Trenton clarified. "The old government's been overthrown by the Resistance with the help of the people. We're all free to leave now if we want. So you could kill me right now, or you could let me go. Think about it, if I'm lying, how did I get all the way out here without getting shot? Has anyone else ever made it this far?"

"Yes. Once. Years ago," Hulk said, but he looked uncertain.

---

[1] That's what Trenton named him as soon as he saw him, and really, what other name could he have?

"One person's made it out here in all these years, and on the night all your buddies left because of an uprising, I just happen to be the second? Seems like a pretty big coincidence."

"How did you know they all left?" Hulk looked no less intimidating standing motionless in the moonlight.

"It's pretty obvious. They would have seen what was happening and would have gone to try and help their friends, who were probably fighting for their lives in the middle of the city. But they wouldn't have left the perimeter completely undefended. Each tower probably has one man left behind to defend it."

"That's what I said we should do, but they thought it was more important to rescue the government. I'm the only one watching these three closest guard towers."

Trenton mentally slapped himself in the face as hard as he could. "So if I had ran for a different guard tower, I could have slipped in, armed myself and found a way over the wall without anyone ever seeing me."

"Yes."

"So what are you going to do with me?"

"I think I'll just wait for full communications to come back online. I'll see what the person on the other end says I should do."

"How anticlimactic," Trent said. "We'll be sitting around for hours."

"Yes. We might as well go inside while we wait. You first." Hulk circled around behind Trenton, urging him forward with the implicit threat of a bullet to the backside.

From the inside, the tower was *far* more welcoming. They walked into a narrow corridor that appeared to be have an opening up above for guards to rain hell down on any intruders. From there, they made their way into a small kitchen, and in the second he had to look around, Trent noted the distinct lack of potential weapons. Trenton moved to sit down on a plain metal stool, but was sharply reprimanded. "Keep walking!" Hulk bellowed[1]. Hoping to avoid provoking the man any further, Trent readily complied, leaving the kitchen and finding his way into a room full of blank holographic screens.

"I'm guessing this is where you watch the barrier and everything else." He stood, waiting for the command to sit after how badly that had went last time.

---

[1] Roid rage is no joke kids.

Hulk didn't speak, just took Trent's backpack; all Trenton heard was some rustling and shuffling as Hulk settled into a chair and rummaged through the bag before dumping it unceremoniously onto the ground. He sat behind Trenton, out of sight, gun surely still pointed at Trenton's comparably tiny figure. Trent searched the room for a weapon but nothing viable was in sight, let alone within reach.

I need to try something. *If I don't, I'm dead anyways once the rest of The Program comes back online.* Out loud he said, "Can I sit down now, or am I going to have to stand for hours while the new government gets their act together?"

Hulk uttered a non-committal grunt.

"Ok, I'm sitting down. Please refrain from shooting me." Trent inched his way towards a chair and perched on the edge of the seat. No bullet tore through him, so he had that to be thankful for.

He positioned his body so that he was facing the array of screens, with Hulk just visible off to his left. Trent tried to start a conversation, to distract the man even a little, but was told unceremoniously to "Shut the fuck up, please."

They passed the next hour in silence. Trenton was growing increasingly anxious as time went by, but from the outside tried to maintain an unaffected appearance. He made note of the two doors on the far side of the room. Maybe something useful was behind one of them. Finally, he decided to try the oldest trick in the "How to Escape Your Capturer" book: the bathroom break.

"If I sit here any longer I think I'm going to piss my pants. Is there a bathroom in this place?"

Frowning[1], Hulk stared him down. "No."

"No?" Trenton repeated, incredulous. "What do you mean 'no'? There's no bathroom here?"

"There's a bathroom. But you're not using it. You can piss your pants."

Trent bit down on his tongue to avoid launching himself at Hulk right then and there. Luckily for him, his will to live was stronger than his boiling anger. But only just. When his temper cooled a little, he resumed his search for another way out. He spent another 29 minutes thinking and came up with nothing. In a few more hours, the sun would rise, and any chance of escaping would be lost forever.

---

[1] He seemed to do that a lot. Seemed to enjoy it even.

This was it. There were no other options. There was no way he was leaving this room unless he did something drastic. So he concentrated, waited for the liquid to move through his body, and emptied the substantial contents of his bladder as he sat nonchalantly in the chair. It darkened his pants, ran down his leg, splattered the chair and pooled on the tiled floor.

"The hell?" Hulk noticed what Trenton was doing and shot to his feet. "Get up!" He yelled. Trenton happily complied.

"I'm not taking you to the bathroom, you piece of shit. You can stand in your own piss for the rest of the night." Hulk seemed to be able to put more words together when he was provoked. "First, you're gonna clean this up."

He prodded Trent's back with the barrel of the machine gun, herding him towards the kitchen. Trenton looked around the countertops again but there were no potential weapons sitting out. A knife would be best, but he'd have to settle for anything he could find. If he could manage to even look in a drawer without getting shot, that is.

Hulk kept the pressure of the gun firm between Trent's shoulder blades. "Under the sink. Get the cleaner." The neurons in Trent's brain fired, creating a new connection, and Trent looked towards the three stools positioned before the counter to his left. He examined their base, but was unsure whether they were attached to the floor.

To avoid drawing Hulk's suspicion, he quickly bent down in front of the sink and opened the cabinet. He removed the spray cleaner and turned around as he stood back up. Hulk was still there with his hulking weapon. After another frown, Hulk stepped aside and allowed Trenton to move past him.

Trenton leaned on the first stool as he went by, and felt it give slightly under his hand. The gun was still wedged comfortably into his back. The second stool he ignored, but as he reached the last chair, he dropped the cleaner and grabbed the chair with both hands, swinging it in arc behind him. He turned with it, heard the scream of the gun as it came to life, felt the jolt as the stool collided with the side of Hulk's head, bringing him to the floor. He felt the heat of the machine gun on his palms as he wrestled with the somehow still conscious beast. He kneed the man once in the stomach – it felt like kneeing a boulder – as the gun continued to fire into the space around them.

They were still struggling when the weapon coughed and ran dry. They both stopped for a second and stared at each other and down at the gun. Then Trent kneed Hulk in the groin, wrested the gun from the man's hands, and smashed his head in with it repeatedly until Hulk's eyes stared blankly up at him, a small frown still plastered on his pale face. Shaking with adrenaline and disgust, Trent rose to his feet, shocked by the amount of blood that covered the body and floor. He stared down at Hulk's motionless form for another two seconds, curious about the source of the blood – the crushed head wasn't bleeding nearly enough to have made such a mess - before turning away.

It was only then that he noticed the sharp pain in his side – a bullet had ripped through right below his ribs. If he had turned even a millisecond faster, the bullet would have missed him completely. But if he had turned any slower, he'd probably be dead. As it was, it was only an inch from his side, which seemed as good a place as any to get shot. He took a step in the direction he imagined the bathroom to be – and nearly collapsed as a wave of dizziness crashed down on him.

He was bleeding from both his front and back on the same side, which hopefully meant the bullet had traveled clean through. Staggering back into the room where he had pissed himself, he clasped one hand on the entry wound and one hand on the exit. Feeling the torn, blood-soaked fabric of his shirt against his hands, the impossibility of his current situation caused him to gasp out a laugh.

He moved gingerly towards the closer of the two doors he had seen earlier, hoping it was the bathroom, and that they kept first aid supplies there.

It *did* turn out to be a bathroom. Too bad it didn't contain even one shitty bandage. Trenton was tempted to look upstairs, but doubted his ability to make it to the top in his current state. Instead he cleaned out his wounds as best he could (so not very well), and tied a spare towel tightly around his stomach, covering both of his brand new bullet holes.

There must be some way to reach the outside of the wall from the tower in case there's an attack or someone escapes. This tower is embedded in the wall after all. The other side must look out on the land beyond the city. I'll check the rest of the bottom floor and then crawl up the stairs if I have to, he thought, despite the fact that he had no idea how he would manage to reach the ground on the other side if the only way out was on the second floor or higher.

A sound interrupted his thoughts and Trenton looked up involuntarily, directly into his own face, which was staring back at him from deep within the bathroom mirror. He had avoided examining this broken visage too closely until this point, but now he forced himself to look, momentarily forgetting the sound that had caused him to look up in the first place.

What he saw did not appall him given all the twisted crap he'd done and had done to him (and to his face). His nose was bent at an odd angle, still broken from the first of his two fights of the night. His shower in his apartment – likely his last shower for a while – had washed away all the blood, but by now he was sweating and some fresh spatters of red – probably spray from bashing in Hulk's head - ornamented his face. Yet still, the green eyes in the mirror looked no different to him, even after all he had done. He wasn't sure if that meant he hadn't changed, or he had changed so much that he couldn't even recognize that he had[1].

A low murmur snuck in through the cracks in the door and broke Trenton out of his philosophical contemplation. Noiselessly, Trent moved to the half-open bathroom door, peeking out into the adjacent room containing the set of blank screens. They were now showing footage of the areas surrounding the wall, with one screen showing a panel of people asking questions of the Savior himself. That explained the voices he had heard. The Program was back up and running. It also meant he better get his ass in gear, bullet wound or not.

He checked the second door in the room: a closet. Fantastic. He gathered up his backpack and patted himself on the back for packing so light. If it had been any heavier he wouldn't have been able to carry it. *Guess it's time to try the stairs.* With growing trepidation, he hobbled onto the first step. He grabbed tightly to the railing and climbed another stair, each move inciting a fresh surge of spinning in his head and burning in his side.

Trenton made it more than halfway up the first flight before he fell (forward thankfully). At the last second, he managed to brace himself with his forearms, avoiding what would have been an excruciatingly painful encounter between his broken nose and the metal steps. He paused for a second to allow his head to settle and his strength to return. When neither of those things happened, he started to crawl up the stairs anyways.

---

[1] i.e., gone crazy.

The last step was particularly difficult for no other reason than Trenton's reserves of strength seemed to have been wrung dry. He tottered on all fours, the weight of his backpack almost pulling him backwards before he righted himself and flopped onto the flat ground of the second floor.

The room was fading in and out, and Trent was reminded of the considerable amount of blood he had already lost. "Should probably eat a protein bar or something," he mumbled to the room. But there were no protein bars; there was no food at all, at least none visible from Trent's position on the floor. He thought of the kitchen downstairs and wondered if any of those cabinets hid any snacks. "Too late now." A second later, his muddled mind remembered the backpack he was still carrying. He slipped it off, and pulled out – yes – a protein bar.

Knowing that to stop moving would mean sure death, Trenton fought his way to his knees and with the support of the wall, proceeded to push himself all the way to his feet. He gnawed on the bar as he inched down the hallway with one hand on the wall, and entered the first room that he encountered.

The room was dark, and Trenton experienced a moment of increased agony as his body tensed in the search for the light. When his hand found the switch and lit up the room, Trent stared at the newly revealed unkempt bed with undisguised longing. But no windows looked out over the wall, and Trenton quickly (for someone who needed to crawl up stairs at least) moved on. He polished off the rest of the protein bar and the world stopped spinning quite so much.

The second room in the hallway opened up to reveal another control-like room. Numerous displays filled the room, their screens illuminated with images of the areas near the barrier, but more importantly, past the screens *was a window*. Trenton approached the glass slowly, half due to his wound, and half out of fear. What if it didn't lead to the other side of the wall, or even if it did, how was he going to get through it and safely to the ground? It took him nearly a minute to move the twenty-one feet from the door to the far wall.

Outside, the sky was turning a lighter shade of gray as the sun prepared its ascent. Trenton looked down to the ground, and took in his first real sight of the world beyond the City. It was decidedly ordinary, more forests and fields. But it instilled in him a sense of wonder he hadn't felt since before his mother had tried to leave and the world had turned to shit. He turned his attention to the window itself, looking for any way to open it – there was none. Down below, he heard a door creak open and the muffled pounding of boots on the tiled floor.

Trenton kicked out at the window, triggering no response besides a flare of pain in his side. Shouted commands floated up to him, indicating the guards were in the process of securing the last of the first floor rooms. Dredging up the very last of his will, he backed up and ran at the window, turning his shoulder into it as he made contact. The pain in his side erupted and the glass barely vibrated in reply. He groaned in pain, sliding to the floor. Hearing more sounds from below, he attempted to rise, getting no more than a few inches before collapsing back to the ground. Few thoughts fought for attention in his head; calmness descended upon him.

Free from worry, he gazed out over the apathetic forest that lay just beyond reach and waited for the sun to rise.

THE END

www.ingramcontent.com/pod-product-compliance
Lightning Source LLC
Chambersburg PA
CBHW070934130626
46555CB00001B/432